She went to the doorway and took Eliza by her shoulders. "But you mind what I tell you. Something in this house is watching us, and its thoughts are not kindly. It's all twisted up and bitter inside. It means to make us suffer. Then it means to kill us, one by one . . ."

## ABOUT THE AUTHOR

Donald Tyson is a Canadian from Halifax, Nova Scotia. After graduating with honors as an English major, he has pursued a writing career. His books include *Ritual Magic*, *Rune Magic*, and *The New Magus*, but his very first published work was a horror story in *Rod Serling's Twilight Zone Magazine*. Tyson's goal is to formulate an accessible system of personal training composed of East and West, past and present, that will help people discover the purpose for their existence as well as ways to fulfill it.

## TO WRITE TO THE AUTHOR

If you wish to contact the author or would like more information about this book, please write to the author in care of Llewellyn Worldwide and we will forward your request. Both the author and publisher appreciate hearing from you and learning of your enjoyment of this book and how it has helped you. Llewellyn Worldwide cannot guarantee that every letter written to the author can be answered, but all will be forwarded. Please write to:

Donald Tyson
c/o Llewellyn Worldwide
P.O. Box 64383-836, St. Paul, MN 55164-0383, U.S.A.

Please enclose a self-addressed, stamped envelope for reply, or $1.00 to cover costs.
If outside U.S.A., enclose international postal reply coupon.

## FREE CATALOG FROM LLEWELLYN

For more than 90 years Llewellyn has brought its readers knowledge in the fields of metaphysics and human potential. Learn about the newest books in spiritual guidance, natural healing, astrology, occult philosophy and more. Enjoy book reviews, new age articles, a calendar of events, plus current advertised products and services. To get your free copy of the *New Times*, send your name and address to:

*The Llewellyn New Times*
P.O. Box 64383-836, St. Paul, MN 55164-0383, U.S.A.

A Llewellyn Psi-Fi Novel

# THE MESSENGER

Donald Tyson

1993
Llewellyn Publications
St. Paul, Minnesota, 55164-0383, U.S.A.

Cover Painting by Martin Cannon
Design by Christopher Wells

**Library of Congress Cataloging-in-Publication Data**

Tyson, Donald, 1954–
    The messenger / Donald Tyson.
        p. cm. — (Llewellyn's psi-fi series)
    ISBN 0–87542–836–3 : $4.99
    1. Occultism—Nova Scotia—Fiction.   I. Title.
    II. Series
PR9199.3.T94M47   1993
823'.914—dc20                                    93-26249
                                                 CIP

Llewellyn Publications
A Division of Llewellyn Worldwide, Ltd.
P.O. Box 64383, St. Paul, MN 55164-0383

Llewellyn's
**Psi-Fi**
Series

## Announcing Llewellyn's FICTION Line

Llewellyn Publications launches its new line of occult fiction with two titles by best-selling authors of the supernatural: Raymond Buckland and Donald Tyson. Intriguing and entertaining, the books in this series are also highly educational because they are based on authentic and accurate metaphysical practices, written by world-recognized experts in the occult. Look for exciting new additions to the line in the upcoming months.

## THE MESSENGER

Sealed inside a secret room of an old mansion in Nova Scotia is a cruel and uncontrollable entity, created years earlier by an evil magician. When the new owner of the mansion unknowingly releases the entity, it renews its malicious and murderous rampage. Called on to investigate the strange phenomena are three women and four men—each with their own occult talents. As their investigation proceeds, the group members enters into a world of mystery and horror as they encounter astral battles, spirit possession—even death. In their efforts to battle the evil spirit, they use seance, hypnotic trance and magical rituals, the details of which are presented in fascinating and accurate detail.

## Other Books by Donald Tyson

*The New Magus*, 1988
*Rune Magic*, 1988
*The Truth About Ritual Magic*, 1989
*The Truth About Runes*, 1989
*How to Make and Use a Magic Mirror*, 1990
*Ritual Magic*, 1991

## Editor and Annotator

*Three Books of Occult Philosophy Written by Henry
    Cornelius Agrippa von Nettesheim*, 1993

## Cards and Kits

*Rune Magic Deck*, 1988
*Power of the Runes*, 1989

*And lest I should be exalted above measure
through the abundance of the revelations,
there was given to me a thorn in the flesh,
the messenger of Satan to buffet me,
lest I should be exalted above measure.*
—II Corinthians 12:7

1

The dry squeal of brakes and the gritting of gravel under the tires of the bus drew Eliza Grey out of her romance paperback.

"Regret Cove," the driver said in a bored voice without turning his head.

She wiped the mist from the inside of her window with a red wool mitten. A transparent oval face with a tapered chin and a small frowning mouth stared back from the wet glass. For a moment it was the face of a frightened child, its eyes sad and its pale brow knitted with strain. Then it became her own face, familiar and plain. In the forgiving glass she looked half her twenty-three years. And felt it, she thought. Self-consciously she tucked a vagrant curl of honey-brown hair back under her red beret.

Beyond her reflection the brooding evergreens guarded the highway like frozen sentinels and shrouded the hunched shoulder of the mountain beyond. It had started to snow. Tiny crystals

1

slanting from the slate sky merged the forest into one indistinct dark mass.

Thrusting her book into the baggy folds of her leather purse, she advanced to the front of the bus.

"Driver, there must be some mistake. Regret Cove is a fishing village."

He looked her up and down, then nodded toward his side window.

"Down that road."

Peering past his head, she saw that a narrow rutted dirt track diverged from the highway and disappeared in a downward slope among the spruce trees. It was not visible from her seat on the other side of the bus.

Surprise made her hesitate. She had expected to find Professor Hale waiting for her, or at least to be dropped off in a town. This was the middle of nowhere.

"Are you gettin' off, girlie?"

Nervously she glanced at the beige travel case beside her seat. A mother and her little girl three places behind the driver watched her with solemn eyes. The rest of the seats were vacant.

"I don't know, it's not what I expected..."

By reflex she reached out with her mind. The frustration boiling inside the driver made her flinch. She saw his knuckles whiten on the steering wheel.

"You want out or not?" he said, arching his eyebrows and smiling tightly at her.

"Couldn't you wait while I ..."

He sighed as though the weight of the over-hanging mountains rested on his narrow shoulders and jerked off the parking brake without answering.

"Stop! Stop the bus! I'm getting off."

She hurried back to her seat for her suitcase and pushed her way out the side door. The bus rattled around the bend in a blue cloud of gas fumes. For almost a minute she stood listening to its diminishing engine sound.

Silence settled over the forest like a soft kiss. Eliza brushed a crystal of snow from the long, straight bridge of her nose and turned the fur collar of her camel-hair coat up around her ears. She had never felt so alone, so completely vulnerable. With reluctant steps she crossed the highway and started down the side road.

After the rush and roar of Toronto the transition to northern Cape Breton was like a journey back in time. The nearer she got to her destination, the more primitive the mode of travel. From Toronto to Halifax she had flown in a sleek commercial jet, then from Halifax to Sydney in a smaller passenger prop. A modern touring bus had taken her from Sydney to the northern tip of the Highlands. There she had managed to find the rickety local bus to carry her to Regret Cove, where Hale had promised to meet her.

A good thing I wore practical boots with flat heels, she thought as she picked her way over the frozen ridges of the mud ruts. Already the fine blowing snow had covered the bottoms of the hollows and made walking treacherous.

It was a crazy way to spend her Christmas holiday. Three months ago while safely cradled in the warm, fuzzy cocoon of academic life she had run across Hale's ad in the University Of Toronto newspaper:

> Wanted! Serious graduate or under-graduate students with occult or para-normal abilities to accompany noted parapsychologist on field trip. Purpose, to investigate phenomena surrounding historic haunted site in northern Nova Scotia, Canada. Duration, Dec. 23–Jan. 2. Students to pay own travel expenses. Room and board provided on site. By special arrangement students who complete this seminar will be awarded half a university credit. Contact Dr. Ebenezer Hale, Dept. of Psychology, University of Colorado. Qualified applicants only!

At the time she was thoroughly sick of the hothouse environment of campus life and longed for a break in the grinding monotony of library research. Her graduate thesis on the juvenilia of the Brontë sisters had reached a dead end. Depression held her mind in an iron grip. She even considered abandoning university for a regular job in the hope that it would shake her from the dull waking dream into which she had fallen. With the money from her portion of her father's estate nearly eaten up by tuition fees and rent, she would soon have to look for work in any case. The sheer craziness of the ad appealed to her romantic temperament.

The reputation of Ebenezer Hale kept her from dismissing the seminar as just another crackpot project. His latest best-selling book on poltergeists had been made into a six-part miniseries for public television. He was rapidly becoming the paranormal guru of the network news and talk-show circuit. Whenever there was a reported miracle, or a UFO close encounter, or a sighting of Bigfoot, the media sought Hale's opinion. Somehow he was able to maintain the difficult balance between popularity and academic respectability.

Much to her surprise, her application was accepted. Hale sent a curt letter of directions in his own handwriting instructing Eliza to meet him in Regret Cove on the twenty-third of December. The letter provided no additional information about the seminar. She had tried several times to reach him by telephone without success. Now here she was on a lonely forest track with no idea of where she was going or what awaited her at the end.

The trees fell away down a steep bank on the left to reveal a small coastal inlet with a haphazard cluster of houses and shacks. Brightly painted fishing boats rocked on the grey water beside a wooden wharf. Other boats rested high and dry on timbers next to the houses. The breeze carried the salt of the open ocean to her nostrils. It was a smell unfamiliar to her midwestern childhood.

As it entered the village the road dropped so steeply Eliza had to slide down part of it to keep from falling. It was impossible to imagine how an automobile could ascend this hill in the spring, yet there were many cars and pickup trucks in front of the houses. Not all of the vehicles were in working order. She passed a dilapidated house with an ancient rusting wringer washing machine in the rocky plot that served for its front yard.

So this is where Buicks come to die, she thought to herself.

It was not what she had expected. The village was little more than a straggle of houses perched precariously on top of the rocks. It had no center. Eliza had assumed there would be a public building of some kind, a post office or a general store, where she could ask after Professor Hale. There was not even a place where she could sit and rest her legs. Wearily she continued down toward the wharf where several men worked around the boats. They eyed her suitcase curiously.

Eliza stopped beside a fisherman who was loading lobster traps into the back of his pickup.

"I wonder if you can help me?"

He banged the tailgate closed with a shower of rust and turned. His eyes where the clearest sky blue she had ever seen. They seemed incongruously youthful in his deeply-lined face.

"What do you want?"

"I'm looking for a man named Ebenezer Hale. I was supposed to meet him here today."

"You missed him."

"What?" Eliza stared at him. "What do you mean?"

The fisherman took out a pipe and began to fill its bowl from a foil pouch of cut tobacco.

"Just what I said. He was here not more than two hours ago. Paid me to take him up the coast in my boat, him and a bunch of others."

"He told me he would meet me," Eliza said, fighting down an irrational panic.

"Guess he figured you weren't coming."

He ignited a wooden match in one hand with the edge of his thumbnail and sucked on the pipe several times. Aromatic smoke puffed from his mouth.

Eliza looked at her watch. It was barely past three in the afternoon. When had Hale expected her to arrive?

"What am I supposed to do now?" she said in desperation.

"I was just going to say," the fisherman continued laconically. "This Hale fella left word I was to bring anyone who showed late on up to Haven after him."

A wave of relief washed over Eliza. She had not been forgotten after all.

"Name's Tim McNeil."

"Eliza Grey."

He wiped the rust from his palm on the thigh of his worn work jeans and shook her hand.

"What is Haven?" she asked curiously. "Another fishing village?"

A young man who stood a few paces away listening to the conversation with his hands in his overalls pockets grinned and spat on the snow-salted planks.

"She'll find out soon enough, but she won't like it much," he muttered to no one in particular.

Several other men laughed and averted their eyes from her.

"Shut your mouth, Elmore," McNeil said.

He picked up Eliza's suitcase and put his hand on her shoulder to guide her along the wharf.

"Don't pay any attention to Elmore. He's the village idiot. If we're goin', we got to leave right now before the water gets too choppy."

He helped her down into a long open boat with a calloused hand. In moments they were skimming across the ocean. Eliza clung to the gunwales in the bow. Away from the shelter of the shore the sea was rough. A stiff breeze raised whitecaps on the crests of the waves as they rolled toward the rocky coast. The noisy outboard sent the boat skipping forward like a stone.

"Wind's comin' up. Won't be long before the weather turns foul," shouted McNeil from the stern.

He took the pipe from his wind-reddened face and spat over the side, grinning at her pleasantly with tobacco-stained teeth.

She braced her knees and let go with one hand to raise the fur collar of her coat over her right ear. The wind wanted to hold it down. Crystals of ice drove against her cheek like stinging thorns and transformed the forested mountains into menacing giants. For long stretches of the coast there was no place at all to land a boat. The rocky cliffs dropped sheer into the thundering white foam of the breakers.

"You said there were others with Professor Hale. How many others?"

He silently counted to himself with his eyes rolled skyward.

"Four."

She turned back to the sea, and back into herself. Only six of us. She had expected more. Still, it would be easier for her this way. Fewer emotions to deal with.

The boat skipped on steadily for the better part of an hour. The mountains along the shore retreated inland, giving place to low rolling hills and an occasional beach of wave-scoured granite boulders. Not a single habitation broke the dreary, interminable margin of forest.

"Look ahead," the fisherman shouted. "You'll see the place when we round this point."

Eagerly she scanned the ridge of black stone that thrust like a great axe blade into the waves. As the boat curved past it the shore line opened on a small inlet with a crescent pebble beach. The land behind the beach rose in a gentle slope for several hundred yards to the foundation of a large house. It reared up unexpectedly from the frosted lawn as though transported there whole by some druidic magic.

"There she is, Haven By the Sea."

Something in the McNeil's voice caused Eliza to reach back toward him with her mind. Her shoulders stiffened. He was terrified. But why?

There was nothing to cause fear in the dull gray prospect. Just the opposite. The darkly forested hills behind the stony points on either side sheltered the inlet from the wind, lending it a strange stillness. Even the waves became gentle against the boat as they entered it.

Eliza studied with curiosity the place she was to spend the next ten days. The house was a great timber-frame, utterly devoid of the quaint charm that distinguishes most Victorian architecture. Three rows of tall mullioned windows broke the severity of its sheer white face. A wrought-iron parapet ran around the peaked and dormered green copper roof with its many stone chimneys. The central portion formed a pillared portico the windows of which peered at the sea as through a set of white bars. Wings on either side clutched the land with idiot defiance.

As they approached the beach the house appeared to rise up and tower over the boat. The illusion was disturbingly real. Eliza looked back at McNeil. The fisherman nodded.

"Everyone says the same thing first time they see it."

Eliza felt a growing inner tension coupled with a sense of personal significance. This moment was important in her life. She intuited this with a strength that made denial impossible. Somehow Haven would change her irrevocably. But whether the change would be good or evil was not clear. She only knew that she stood at a crossroad. She could remain on the boat and let it carry her back to

Toronto and her dull university grind, or go forward into the unknown.

I won't go back, she told herself firmly. Whatever happens, I won't go back.

**2**

McNeil tied up the boat and helped Eliza onto the icy dock. In the hour it had taken to reach Haven the fine snow, now almost invisible in the fading light, had managed to cover the land with a sandy carpet more than an inch thick.

"Mind your step," he said. "Half the planks are rotted out."

She bent to retrieve her suitcase from the boat but he waved her away.

"You might as well go on up to the hotel. I'll bring your bag and put it in the front hall."

She nodded, feeling a spring of pleasure mingled with relief. Haven must be a vacation resort. A hotel meant staff and other guests. There would be an impersonal human environment to retreat into if the emotions of the group became too intense.

A brick walkway with a series of shallow steps led from the dock to the front entrance, which was terraced with more brick in a herringbone pattern. Eliza kicked through a snow-crusted drift of rustling

12

brown leaves as she approached the door and tried the wrought-iron handle. It would not turn. There was no bell. Clenching her fist inside her mitten, she hit the oak panel. It was like hitting the frozen ground. The door gave back a faint muffled thud.

McNeil was still in the boat with his back to her. She could see him pouring gasoline from a large can into the top of the outboard. Eliza leaned her shoulder against one of the pillars and waited for him to turn around. When he showed no sign of losing interest in the outboard she started to call him, then changed her mind and stepped off the portico to explore around the house.

Its uncurtained windows stared bleakly down like blind eyes as she passed under their sills. Patches of white paint peeling from the clapboards reminded her of sores. The long brown grass on the lawn, beaten over by autumn winds, stuck up through the snow in low looped tufts. Her boots crunched on it. She was forced to walk carefully with her eyes down to keep from tripping.

Shrill laughter floated on the crystalline air from behind the hotel. She rounded the rear corner and looked up. A man and a woman stood some distance apart on the back lawn playing with a bright yellow Frisbee. They were both around her own age. The man jumped with athletic ease to catch the Frisbee and the woman applauded.

"Hello," Eliza called. "Are you with Professor Hale's group?"

He raked melting snow from his curly blond hair with his fingers and walked toward her while the woman stood watching with her hands on her hips.

"Yes we are," he said when he was close enough to extend his hand. "Lee Sheppard."

She pulled off her mitten and took his hand. It was strong and responsive.

"Eliza Grey."

She stared up into his intense blue eyes and forced a slight smile. He had a serious face with clean, rugged features and a cleft chin. His bulky sheepskin jacket did little to conceal the breadth of his shoulders or his lean, muscular body.

For a moment he continued to study her quietly. Then he turned to the woman.

"Amber, come over here and meet a fellow inmate."

The woman let her hands slide from her hips and started toward them. Eliza tried not to gawk at her coat, a luxurious black mink with a broad hood. The shoulder-length auburn hair framing her high Nordic cheekbones and full lips contrasted strikingly with her green eyes, an effect heightened by skillful mascara and deep red lipstick. She moved with animal grace, stepping across the snow-crusted grass with cat-like assurance in spite of the high heels on her black leather fashion boots.

Eliza became acutely conscious of the ragged lining inside her old camel-hair coat. She extended her perception and recoiled inwardly. This woman was hostile.

"Eliza Grey — Amber Fox," Lee said.

The two touched fingers.

"We had nearly given up hope for you," Amber said in a compelling, husky voice.

"I know, I'm late. My bus was delayed."

She's jealous, Eliza realized. Wonderingly she cast a sidelong glance at Lee Sheppard. Bitter amusement welled within her. The jealousy would pass soon enough once Amber came to know her.

"We're glad you made it," Lee said. "We need the company. This place is a mausoleum."

"At least you can laugh at it," Eliza said.

He gave her a quizzical look.

"Well anyway, you were laughing a minute ago."

"We weren't laughing."

She stared at each of them. They met her gaze blankly. Gently she brushed their minds. Lee was puzzled and concerned. Amber's puzzlement was mixed with contempt.

"But I heard laughter. It was loud — you must have heard it."

Both shook their heads.

"You better go inside and describe what you heard to Professor Hale," Lee said. "He'll want to meet you anyway."

"Could you show me —"

"Come on, Lee, let's play," Amber cried, grabbing the Frisbee out of his hand.

She ran lithely over the lawn and Lee stepped forward to follow her. Turning, she flung the yellow plastic disk in a rising arc that passed over his head and descended toward Eliza. The Frisbee skipped off Eliza's fingertips when she reached up to catch it.

A massive shape hurtled through the air past her shoulder. Eliza flinched away instinctively, then relaxed and took a deep breath, exhaling slowly between her lips. An enormous mastiff with short brick-colored fur and floppy ears bounded across the lawn toward Amber with its tail beating from side to side, the Frisbee clamped in its jaws. Amber took back the Frisbee and ruffled the dog's neck, watching Eliza with amusement.

"Luther! Here, boy!"

The command came from the rear door of the hotel. A short powerfully-built man with white hair and a full white beard stood framed in the open doorway. Eliza recognized him at once from his many television appearances. He beckoned to the dog. The mastiff galloped back across the lawn like a pony and disappeared into the hotel. The man turned to Eliza.

"Ms. Grey? Glad you could join us. I'm Ebenezer Hale. The others are inside. You're just in time for our get acquainted session."

He called Lee and Amber over and they followed him into a paneled corridor. Narrow service stairs rose on the left. Beside them was the entrance to the cellar, its plain plank door ajar. A much wider panel door to the right opened on an enormous kitchen with a cast-iron cooking stove. The stove radiated gentle warmth. In the middle of the tiled floor stood a long wooden table. Three people sat around its far end. There were four empty chairs.

They beat the snow and ice from their coats and hung them on a rack behind the kitchen door. Lee's denim shirt and faded jeans matched his comfortable, down-to-earth manner. Beneath the mink Amber wore a pink cashmere sweater and silver metallic ski pants. Strangely enough, this outlandish outfit suited her.

She makes me look as drab as a sparrow standing next to a peacock, Eliza thought.

"The weather here is unpredictable," Hale said in a hearty voice as he brushed off the sleeves of his Icelandic sweater. "Two days ago when I brought in the supplies it was forty-five degrees and the sun was shining. The ground was bare all along the coast. Tonight we're in for a blizzard. It's lucky you all got here before it started. According to McNeil, when the heavy snow comes nothing moves for days."

Hale took his place at the head of the table and gestured for Eliza to sit beside him opposite Lee and Amber.

She cast a curious glance at the other three. Two were men, one a woman. The woman was plain-faced and overweight, with oily brown hair that hung limply over her ears and startled, birdlike brown eyes. She wore a plaid dress of conservative cut, and around her neck a small gold crucifix on a gold chain. One man was an East Indian whose dark hair lay combed flat on his skull, away from his high forehead and hawk-like nose. He had on a burgundy sweater-vest over a white shirt. He nodded politely when her gaze rested on him. The other man was slightly built and pale-skinned with unkempt black hair, prominent ears and a thin nose. The knobs of his shoulders and the sharp ridges of his collar bones were visible under his black pullover. His dark eyes stayed on her while she examined him. They held a subtle humor.

"Eliza Grey," said Hale, "Meet your fellow students Mary Tews, Mohan Singh, and Allan Wibbley."

He pointed to each in turn. She acknowledged their greetings.

"We have no formalities," he went on. "Everyone is on a first name basis. Except for me. You may call me Doctor or Professor or Hale, but never under any circumstance Ebenezer. It makes me sound like something out of Dickens."

"We greet you in this humble chamber," said Allan Wibbley, spreading his thin bony hands to indicate the kitchen, "Not to cast aspersions on your social character, but because it is one of the few warm rooms in this wretched house."

"Is something wrong with the heating?" Eliza asked Hale.

"Not at all. We do what we can with our limited resources."

"Don't the other guests complain?"

Amber laughed.

"There are no others," Lee said. "We're alone."

She remembered the ragged tufts of browning grass and the stark, staring quality of the windows.

"I take it this is the off season."

"Yes," Mohan said with a smile in an accent like softly flowing honey. "It has been off season for a very long time."

"Stop teasing, Mohan. The hotel's closed down," Mary Tews explained to Eliza. Her voice was southern and surprisingly mellow.

"I've been giving the others a few background details while we waited to see if you would come," Hale said. "But you'll be able to catch up after dinner. Right now I have something important to discuss. I'd like your attention for a moment if you don't mind, Allan."

Allan stopped whispering to Amber.

"You have my undivided ear."

The mastiff wandered in and crossed under the table, brushing everyone's legs, then turned in a circle and settled itself beside the stove.

"You all know, more or less, why you are here," Hale said, glancing at each of them. "This seminar involves practical field research of an occult manifestation. It is a credit course, by special arrangement with your various universities. At the end of the ten-day term you will be required to write a paper analyzing our findings. On this you will either receive a pass or a fail — there will be no marks given."

"How long is this paper to be?" said Mary.

"That's up to you."

"May we assume this is the locality of the phenomenon?"

"You may."

Allan rapped a large silver ring on his right index finger nervously against the table.

"Just what sort of thing are we dealing with? Poltergeist? Ghost?"

"I don't know."

They all stared at him.

"When I began arranging the details of this seminar I knew almost nothing about the scope or nature of the manifestations at Haven. Since then I have learned a great deal — I'll be giving you the details later tonight — but I still have no idea as to the root cause. That's why you're all here."

He shoved his chair out from the table. The dog looked up, then settled its head on its forepaws. Hale walked around the chair and flexed his short, powerful fingers on its wooden back.

"You were chosen from a field of over three hundred applicants because of your unique individual talents. Each of you is highly proficient in some branch of the occult."

They exchanged glances across the table. They're each wondering what makes the others special, Eliza thought.

"I'll go clockwise around the table," Hale said. "Eliza is an English Major from the University of Toronto. She is an empath. Is there anyone unfamiliar with the term?"

Mohan raised his hand.

"An empath is one who senses the internal emotional states of others. Empath. Short for empathic. Eliza cannot read thoughts but she reads feelings with remarkable accuracy. I chose her for this seminar because it is vital that I know the stresses building up in each of you, and how close you are to your breaking point."

Eliza sensed a burning and looked across the table at Amber. Amber was staring at her. Eliza felt her cheeks redden.

"Mary," Hale went on, "Is a psychometrist and channeler. She is sensitive to atmospheres and objects. She can communicate with entities beyond the range of our normal human senses. Mary is a nutritionist on loan to us from Indiana State.

"Mohan was completing his doctoral thesis on comparative religion at Harvard when I persuaded him to join us. He is skilled in the discipline of kundalini yoga. I am hoping that his Eastern perspective will give us unexpected insights into the nature of the occurrences at Haven.

"Allan —" Hale paused and frowned. "Well, what can I say about Allan. He is attending an Arts program at the University of Nebraska, but his true vocation is goetic thaumaturgy."

"What on earth is that?" Eliza said.

"I conjure demons," Allan told her with a crooked smile. "Isn't that so, Professor."

"Allan is skilled in the manipulation of self-aware spiritual entities that sometimes involve themselves maliciously in human affairs."

"Demons," Allan breathed, winking at Eliza.

"As for Amber," Hale continued around the table, "She is in her senior year at Radcliffe, and an hereditary witch. I selected her because it is possible that the forces we are dealing with at

Haven By the Sea are below the level of intellec-
tual and symbolic control. Witchcraft is largely an
intuitive skill relying on the simplest of tools and
methods."

"We witches feel deeply," Amber said to
Eliza, her green eyes widening.

"Finally, Lee comes to us from a small college
in upper state New York called the Phoenix Institute. It is devoted exclusively to occult studies and
is well respected by those who understand its aims.
Lee is a Hermetist."

Several faces went blank.

"A follower of the teachings of Hermes Tris-
megistus," Lee explained.

"Lee is skilled in a broad range of subjects
that include astrology, numerology, runes, the
Tarot, the practical Kabbalah, alchemy and ritual
magic. I wanted him along because he has a bal-
anced overview of the occult. His background may
help us solve any problems that arise."

Eliza gazed out the fly-specked kitchen windows at the falling snow. She shivered in spite of
the warmth from the stove. The gloom thickened
by the minute. Yesterday had been the winter sol-
stice, the shortest day of the year when the sun
withholds its sustaining radiance and life reaches
its lowest ebb.

Hale leaned forward and rested his elbows on
the back of the chair. His expression became serious.

"It is no coincidence that this seminar falls on
the Christmas hiatus. It is during this time that the
phenomena at Haven reach their peak. If I had

known all I know now when I was planning this field trip I might never have pursued it to realization. I won't lie to you. There's danger here, mortal physical danger. Men and women have died within these walls at the hands of the forces we seek to investigate."

He paused to let his words sink home. The dog whined in its sleep. Its paws began to twitch.

"If any of you wish to leave I will understand. McNeil has instructions to hold the boat. It won't depart until I give the order. But once it does leave there is no calling it back. It won't return until the second of January. There's no road and the nearest house is more than thirty miles through trackless mountain woods."

"What if there's a medical emergency?" Mary said. "How will we get help?"

"I have a battery powered short-wave radio upstairs," said Hale. "I will use it in the case of a life-threatening emergency, but only in that case. I warn you, I will not be moved by second thoughts, vain regrets or idle misgivings."

He pushed himself erect and picked at the elbows of his sweater.

"I'm sorry. I know you should be given all the facts before you're forced to make a decision, but there just isn't time. A storm is blowing up. I have to release the boat within the next few minutes."

He waited, watching them.

He's holding something back, Eliza thought. Gently she probed Hale's emotions. He was stalking them like a mischievous boy hunting a bird. He knew something important, but he didn't want to tell them for fear it would frighten them away.

"I don't know about the rest of you," Allan said, "But I've seen things that would probably make whatever's haunting this hotel run for its mother. I'll stay."

"Count me in," Amber said, a note of challenge in her deep voice.

"I will remain," said Mohan.

"Me too, I guess," Mary piped. "Hope I don't live to regret it."

"I'm staying," Lee said quietly. "What about you, Eliza?"

Eliza met his eyes. He was so cool inside, so poised.

"I'm with you."

Hale relaxed. Eliza felt his relief flow across her mind like a spring breeze.

"I'll send the boat away. We'll get our gear stowed and eat. There's more work to be done in one or two of the bedrooms. After that I'll tell you all about Haven."

## 3

"A fair meal, even if it did come out of a can," Hale said, pushing back his empty plate. "We'll leave the washing up until tomorrow, I think. We can take turns each morning in the alphabetical order of last names."

"That means I'm first," Amber objected indignantly.

"Look on the bright side," said Allan. "After tomorrow you'll have the rest of the week free."

There was general nervous laughter. They were still uncertain of each other, but growing more relaxed all the time.

The remainder of the afternoon had been spent filling glass oil lamps, fueling the kerosene heaters upstairs in the bedrooms, making up the beds, and stacking wood for the kitchen stove and the fireplace of the gathering room established by Hale in the front of the house. These tasks were of primary importance. Haven had no electricity. Hale explained that the diesel generator installed in an out building by the last owners to power the lights had seized up from lack of use. Afterwards they busied themselves sorting the boxes of supplies dumped by Hale in the pantry. These consisted mainly of tinned foods, condensed milk, powdered eggs, dried fruits, instant coffee, tea, large cans of kerosene and spare batteries for the flashlights. There had been little time to discuss the reason for coming to Haven.

Darkness shrouded the brooding hills outside. Two kerosene lamps shed wavering puddles of yellow light over the kitchen table and lit the faces of those seated around it from underneath, lending them a macabre appearance. From time to time a puff of wind hurled a fistful of ice pellets at the black panes of glass above the double porcelain sink.

Hale took one of the lamps from the table.

"Let's go into the gathering room. I have several things to show you."

He waited while the others lit lamps they had previously made ready, then led them out of the kitchen along the paneled passage past the formal dining room on the left and into the cavernous front hall.

We look like a chain of lost souls, Eliza thought, following at the end of the line. Shadows from the flickering lamps in front of her slithered eerily over the walls. When they emerged into the great hall it was like entering a dark cathedral. Their footsteps on the flagstone floor sent echoes rattling through the silence.

A carved stone fireplace tall enough to walk into without stooping dominated the space under the second floor balcony. Mounted over it was the head of a stag. In the corner by the front door stood the reception desk, its pale maple front out of place against the darker oak wall panels. Opposite the desk a staircase curved up to the balcony. Doors opened into the wings of the house on either side. A great brass and crystal chandelier hung low over the center of the hall. The ceiling was lost in shadow.

Hale led them to his right past the dark mouth of the fireplace toward the entrance to the east wing. As he paused to pull the heavy oak door open, Mary gasped and almost dropped her lamp. Eliza felt sympathetic needles of shock from the other woman.

"What is it, Mary?" Hale said sharply.

Mary stared wide-eyed, unable to speak.

"There's a face hovering over you," Lee said in a deliberately even tone.

"I see it also," said Mohan in a hushed voice.

Hale looked above his shoulder, then chuckled. Stepping back, he raised his lamp over his head. Above the door was an oil portrait of an elderly man. The background of the painting was dark and the face pale, making it stand forth strangely in the feeble light.

"Daniel P. Brannon, the man who built Haven," Hale explained. "I'm surprised you didn't notice it before."

The features of the face in the portrait were square and strong, the chin jutting, the lips com-

pressed and bloodless, the dark eyes intense
behind half-lowered lids. Eliza shivered as she
looked at it. The face was that of a man accustomed
to getting his own way.

She felt whispers of pain emanating from
someone and noticed Mary holding her hand to
her lips.

"What is it?" she said, touching the other
woman. "Are you hurt?"

"It's nothing," Mary said. "I burned myself
when I caught the lamp shade. Silly of me. It's
nothing."

"I have some ointment in the gathering
room," Hale said.

They passed under the picture into a long corridor and entered the first door on the left. It
opened on a spacious chamber with light oak pan-
eling and a rose-colored marble fireplace. Some
attempt had been made to put it into living order.
A long table occupied the space under the pair of
tall windows in the exterior wall. Around the fireplace were grouped a red leather couch and several
padded armchairs. Opposite the fireplace a rolltop
desk stood against the wall. It was strewn with
papers. Boxes and bags littered two smaller tables
and spilled over onto the oak floor, the bareness of
which had been covered by a faded oriental rug.

"I had McNeil help me cart this stuff down
from the third level. It was hard work, I can tell you."

Hale went to the fireplace and stirred the
ashes with a poker while the others made themselves at home. Sparks flickered up the chimney. In

a few minutes split sections of hardwood were blazing on top of the exposed embers. While Hale puttered with the fire the others helped themselves to a rust-colored liquor in an antique crystal decanter on an end table. Eliza poured some into one of the waiting glasses and tasted cautiously. Scotch.

Allan and Amber settled side by side on the leather couch with an arm around each other. Amber kicked off her boots and stretched her legs luxuriously, admiring the play of firelight on her silver ski pants. Allan raised his glass to the flames and peered through it.

"Things are looking up," he said.

"I brought that bottle along to break the ice," Hale muttered as he sorted through the papers on the rolltop desk. "Enjoy it—it's the only one. I don't want any of my students drunk."

Eliza poured some of the liquor into a clean glass and carried it to the table, where Lee was treating Mary's burn with the first-aid kit.

"Here," she said gently. "Drink this. It will ease the pain."

Mary fingered the crucifix around her neck.

"That's kind of you—but I don't drink."

"This is for medicinal purposes," said Lee. "As your doctor I insist."

"Well—" She sipped the scotch and rolled it on her tongue. A look of surprise came into her face. "It's good."

"Indeed it is," Allan said. "Gloriously good."

Hale handed each of them a set of papers stapled together at the corner.

"I had this copied before coming out here. It contains the background information I'm about to give you. Use it for reference."

He went to the fireplace and rested his elbow on the corner of the scalloped marble mantel.

"You've already met the author of this house. Daniel P. Brannon was a successful American industrialist who made his fortune in coal and steel during the last century. By all accounts he was the original robber baron. He moved into stock speculation and tripled his wealth, then apparently became a philanthropist. He was one of those enigmatic men who spend half their lives making money and the other half giving it away."

"Judging by his portrait, I doubt generosity was one of his vices," Allan said.

"None the less, he built a number of public structures and founded several charities. In 1882 he came to Nova Scotia and built Haven By the Sea as a kind of retreat for himself and his family. The design is his own. He used mostly local materials and workers. Apart from occasional hunting parties Haven served as a summer cottage."

"Some cottage," Eliza murmured.

"Then around the turn of the century Brannon moved here full time. My details of this period are unclear. Apparently Brannon's wife died, and then his only son. The death of his son must have been a heavy blow for the old man. He lived on for another decade almost as a recluse. One morning in 1911 he was found dead in his bed by a servant."

"Natural death?" Allan said.

"Yes."

"How old was the boy?" Lee asked.

"I'm not sure." Hale flipped through his papers. "Let me see—the boy was thirteen."

"How did he die?" asked Mohan from one of the armchairs.

"Pneumonia. I see what you two are getting at. It's true that poltergeist phenomena are often centered around an adolescent, but I'm afraid in this case it won't work. There were no troubles before or after Michael Brannon's death."

"That's a relief," Mary said. "Poltergeists can be horribly spiteful."

"After Brannon's death his relatives sold Haven to a Canadian named Biddingford, who converted it into an expensive hunting lodge. There were moose and bear in the Cape Breton Highlands in those days—still are, for that matter. Biddingford ran the lodge as a paying proposition until 1943, when a fire gutted much of the west wing."

"What caused the fire?" said Amber, staring past Hale into the flames on the hearth.

"It was a freak accident. Some of you may have discovered that much of the ground floor of the west wing is taken up by a large hall. It was used for celebrations and formal dances. On New Year's Eve, 1943, a party was in progress. The blue spruce tree that had been erected for Christmas was still set up in the center of the hall. Apparently it was knocked over in the excitement by some of the guests and fell into the fireplace. It must have been dry as paper. In minutes the room was filled with smoke. The colored cotton hangings and banners mounted over the doors fell burning on the guests as they tried to escape. Many were burned to death. Others were crushed or trampled."

They were silent as Hale paused to consult his notes. The deliberately subdued description of the scene could not disguise its horror. Alive to such things, Eliza felt the tension of the others.

"Biddingford died in a heroic effort to put out the fire. The lodge was boarded up and remained that way for over thirty years. The trustees were unable to find a legitimate buyer. Then in 1975 Haven was sold to a consortium of professional people in Toronto who were looking for a tax shelter. They renovated it, repaired the fire damage, and opened it as a vacation resort in the spring of the following year. The idea was to run it all year round—in summer for fishing and boating, in winter for cross-country skiing and hunting.

"The summer season passed more or less without incident. In the fall strange occurrences began. The owners found they couldn't keep the staff, even after they offered generous increases in salary. The maids complained of being spied on and tormented. The grounds-keepers said that something was following them as they made their rounds."

"In what way were the maids tormented?" asked Mohan.

Hale shrugged and stepped in front of the fireplace, standing with his back to the flames to warm himself.

"The information I have is unclear. As you can imagine, none of them bothered to write their stories down. Everything is hearsay, with the exception of a single firsthand account that I'll get to in a minute. According to the stories the maids would put something down, then turn around to discover it was no longer there. They would make up a room, and minutes later return to find it a shambles. They were convinced that some maniac was creeping through hidden passages and deliberately harassing them. At least, that was one of the explanations given.

"In early winter a major incident took place. Several horses were kept in an out building that had been converted into a stable. One morning they were found dead in their stalls. There were no external marks or signs of injury. They seemed to have died of some sort of fit. Their limbs were contorted, and the boards of the stalls were kicked out."

"Where's Luther?" Eliza said suddenly.

"Probably exploring," said Hale. "I'll call him."

He pursed his lips and let out a low sustained whistle. They listened in silence for several seconds. A clicking noise came from the passage and grew louder. The big mastiff rounded the corner of the open door and trotted over to the hearth, where it sat on its haunches looking expectantly around. Hale ruffled the short red hairs along the dog's thick neck.

"He's a loveable mutt," Hale said. "But I didn't bring him along out of sentiment. Animals have senses that are more acute than ours. Maybe even than yours, Mary."

"Are we to understand that these incidents intensified as the year wore on?" asked Lee.

"As I told you, they seem to peak near the Christmas season and climax with the turning of the year."

"Were any people hurt?" Mary asked hesitantly.

Hale left the fireplace and sat on the rounded arm of couch.

"Unfortunately, yes. Over New Year's several guests were found dead. One woman took an overdose of pills. A man was discovered at the bottom of the main staircase, but the body bore no signs of injury from a fall. There were others but the records have been whitewashed to protect the feelings of family members."

"If what you told us is true we should be nearing the height of the phenomena," Allan said. He spread his hands. "Nothing has happened."

"Yes, that is disturbing, I grant you," said Hale, lacing a finger through his snowy beard.

"It's watching us," Mary said.

They turned to look at her. She sat leaning forward in her chair by the conference table, back rigid, eyes wide and focused on infinity. Hale raised an eyebrow significantly to the others and went over to her chair. She continued to stare at nothing.

"What do you see, Mary?"

She remained silent and unaware of his presence. He passed his hand several times before her face but she did not respond.

"Eliza, what is she feeling?"

"Fear. Horror." Eliza sharpened the focus of her perception on the other woman. "There's a scream building up inside her."

The channeler closed her eyes and fell limply back. She began to breathe in short, quick gasps, faster and faster until she lost control.

"She's hyperventilating," Lee said.

He pushed Hale out of the way. Taking Mary's bloodless hands and holding them pressed together in his left hand, he made passes over her head and palpitating breast. Slowly she opened her eyes. He fixed his gaze on hers, compelling her to look at him.

"What's he doing?" Amber whispered to Allan.

Hale gave them a warning glance.

After a few moments Mary's breathing slowed and color began to return to her fleshy cheeks. Lee folded her hands in her lap and touched his fingertips to her temples. Her eyes fluttered shut.

"Ask her what she saw," Hale said.

"It could be dangerous."

"Ignorance is dangerous. Ask her."

"Mary," Lee said quietly. "Describe the vision that appeared to you."

Mary began to twitch and start. She leaned back, trying to pull away from his hands.

"It's all right," he said soothingly. "You're safe. My aura surrounds and protects you. Tell me the vision."

"Blood," she muttered. "Blood and madness. Eyes blazing with madness. Strength. A knife rising and falling. Blood everywhere ..."

She lapsed into inarticulate moaning. Lee massaged her temples with his fingers and breathed gently across her eyelids. Her features unknotted and grew placid.

"That's all we'll get," he told Hale. "She's suppressed the rest. I could pull it out of her but it would hurt her, maybe seriously."

"No, leave her. Perhaps it will surface on its own after a night's sleep."

Lee reversed the direction of his hand passes across her body and spoke to her, telling her to wake. Mary opened her eyes.

"I mesmerized you," he told her.

She smiled shyly at Lee.

"I know. I don't mind. I trust you."

"Well," Amber said. "True love."

"Don't be bitchy, my dear," said Allan. "It spoils your mystique."

They broke up the knot they had formed around Mary and returned to their former places.

"Professor," said Eliza hesitantly. "I forgot to mention something earlier."

She told him about the laughter.

"Neither of you heard anything?" Hale asked Lee and Amber.

They shook their heads.

Hale sighed. Putting a hand on the back of his neck, he rolled his head.

"We'll put it in the record. It's getting late. I

was going to give you all some additional information but it'll keep until tomorrow. I want you to turn in and get a good night's sleep. Does each of you have an amulet of protection?"

Amber pointed to a silver crescent that hung over her pink sweater in the hollow between her breasts. Allan held up his right hand to show the arcane design on the face of the ring on his index finger. Mohan merely touched the center of his chest and nodded.

"I don't use physical symbols of protection," Lee said.

"What about you, Mary?" Hale asked.

Mary lifted the gold cross on its chain.

"Will this do?"

"Admirably."

Hale looked at Eliza.

"I don't have anything. I don't care much for jewelry."

"I'll give her something," Lee offered.

"Excellent. Go to bed, all of you. I'll join you shortly—I have a little work to finish."

They wandered into the front hall and mounted the stairs. The upper corridor of the east wing was dusty and the faded flower paper on the walls was beginning to peel at the edges. Hale had furnished seven of the rooms in preparation for their arrival, stapling a file card with a name to each door.

Eliza stopped in front of her name and pulled the key out of the lock, then opened the door and entered. Lee followed her. In addition to the

kerosene heater that glowed at a low setting to take
off the chill, the room held a double four-poster bed
of rich dark mahogany and a small maple chest of
drawers mounted with an oval mirror. Hale had
taken the furniture from the attic as he found it,
and each room was furnished with a quixotic disre-
gard for style.

"Do you have a paper and pen?"

Eliza set her lamp on the chest and
unclasped her suitcase on the bed. She drew from
its depths a spiral notebook and a ballpoint and
gave them to him. He tore a small square from one
of the pages in the notebook and held it and the
pen close to his heart. Closing his eyes, he began
to mutter. He seemed almost to be praying. Eliza
could not distinguish his words. Placing the paper
on the chest of drawers, he drew on it a double
circle with several strange marks between, and in
the center a triangle.

"Have you something you can put this in?
Something you can wear?"

She thought a moment, then slid her watch
from her wrist and held it up by its gold expansion
bracelet.

"Only this," she said. "Will it fit under the
back?"

He took the watch and used her nail file to
pry it open. Folding the charm twice, he pressed it
into the cavity, then put the back on.

"I can't guarantee it'll keep perfect time, but
the pentacle should offer you some protection, if
you can believe in its power."

Eliza looked into his blue eyes. They were so intense yet so far away. He seemed to be looking at a part of her she didn't know about.

After what I saw you do to Mary, I'd believe practically anything."

He smiled.

"I'm right across the hall if you need me."

"Thanks, Lee. Good night."

She watched him disappear behind the door on the other side of the corridor before shutting her own door. Shivering, she changed into blue flannel pajamas patterned with large strawberries, and was thankful for the foresight that had caused her to pack them. They might make her look like a frump, but at least they were warm. In the next room Amber was singing in what sounded like Gaelic. Her husky voice drifted faintly through the wall.

"I look a mess," Eliza muttered, staring in the mirror at her pale travel-weary face. Her hazel eyes were bloodshot and her disordered hair looked several shades darker than its normal golden brown. Dusky hollows had settled in her cheeks.

She took a brush from her suitcase and began angrily tugging at her loose curls, which were a mass of knots and tangles. After a moment she threw down the brush in disgust. Setting the lamp on the floor beside the bed, she climbed between the icy sheets. She began to take off her watch as usual, but something made her hesitate. She slid its expandable bracelet back onto her wrist and leaned down to blow out the lamp.

**4**

She followed a green-gowned male attendant down a windowless corridor with a door at the end. Dusty cobwebs clung in the corners. Damp ran down the mouldy walls. The only light came from a single naked bulb hanging on the end of a frayed electrical cord that crackled and sparked fitfully.

On the wall in a shattered glass case hung a fire axe, its blade dripping with blood. Dimly she heard moans, screams and wild laughter.

She passed a naked boy with a shaved head, his skinny body covered with filth and sores. He reached behind his back for a piece of his own feces and put it into his mouth with a drooling idiot grin. She shrank away to keep from touching him. The attendant took her arm and propelled her unwillingly to the end of the corridor.

"You're mother is waiting," he said, opening the door on darkness.

He winked at her. His face was strong and cruel, the face of Daniel P. Brannon.

The door shut behind her. In the darkened room a gray-haired woman sat in a wooden chair facing the blank wall. She was doing something with her hands in the air. Eliza walked slowly around the chair until she could see the familiar features of her mother.

"I came to visit, mama."

The other woman seemed not to hear. With intense concentration she reached into the air in front of her and picked some invisible particle between her thumb and forefinger, then carefully placed it into a little wooden box in her lap. She wore a dress of the same drab institutional green.

Eliza felt a great sorrow mingled with tenderness. She put her hand on her mother's shoulder.

"What are you doing, mama?"

"Why, I'm picking stars, dear. See all the beautiful stars?"

Eliza bent forward. The dark air glittered with countless tiny points of brightness, like motes of dust caught in a beam of sunlight. They danced and trembled as though alive. She caught her breath at their delicate beauty.

"This box is for you, Eliza."

Her mother extended the wooden box toward her. For some reason she drew back and shook her head.

"Take it," her mother insisted. "Take the pretty box of stars."

Reluctantly Eliza accepted the box and opened it. Bright specks overflowed into her hand. They glittered like sparks. They were burning her,

but she did not wish to drop and lose them on the
floor. She blinked and looked again. Abruptly the
sparks had changed into thousands of tiny red spi-
ders that crawled over her palm and wrist. Their
bites felt like countless hot needles. With a cry of
revulsion she dropped the box and shook the spi-
ders off her hand.

The clanging bell of a fire alarm sounded outside the door.

"Now you've done it," her mother said in a
sad, tired voice. "You'll have to go away. I can't
help you any more."

Thunderous pounding came from the other
side of the door. Frantically Eliza looked around for
a way of escape, and saw a jagged gap in the plaster of the wall that was shaped like the mouth of a
cave. She dashed through just as the door burst
open behind her and ran down the dark tunnel.

Something followed her. She sensed its menace, heard its faint crackling hiss. With arms
stretched out to ward off the hanging cobwebs she
fled through the endless darkness, the unseen horror close at her heels.

At the end of the tunnel shone a light. Eliza
ran toward it. She emerged abruptly into blinding
brightness and stood shielding her face while her
eyes adjusted. She found herself on a vast sundial
shaped like a clock with Roman numerals all
around. The knife-like central marker cast its
shadow edge behind her, cutting completely across
the radius of the dial. The shadow was impenetra-
ble, as deep and cold as a frozen pool. From within

it she heard the same menacing crackle and hiss that had pursued her down the tunnel.

She realized the shadow was moving toward her while she looked at it and took a step back. The black edge crawled after her with increasing speed. Again she stepped away from it, and again. With mounting fear she began to back away around the dial. Some sense warned her with utter certainty that she would die if the shadow touched her skin. Still it moved faster, and faster, until she was running to keep from being overtaken.

Her legs felt heavy. She moved in a maddening slow motion while the shadow swept after her like a black scythe. The Roman numerals on the dial had become dates. She ran past them. December twenty-third, twenty-forth, twenty-fifth ...

She looked back over her shoulder in terror. A great hulking silhouette edged in flickering fire ran after her with loping strides and outspread arms to engulf her. Its icy fingers brushed her back.

Something round turned under her foot and made her stumble to her hands and knees. The floor was littered with bleached human bones. She realized it was a skull that had tripped her. Frantically she tried to scramble to her feet. The bones rolled and slid over each other, throwing her down.

She turned and raised her arm to ward off the fiery shadow. It loomed over her and descended with the voracity of a bird of prey. Terror drained the strength from her limbs. She could not move. She felt a scream rise in her throat.

# 5

The thud of footsteps overhead shocked Eliza from her nightmare. She sat up in bed with a gasp, heart pounding, then forced herself to relax. The sounds were obviously made by human feet, and it was difficult to feel supernatural dread with the clear light of morning filling the room. She glanced at her watch. It had continued to run, and showed nearly nine o'clock.

Quickly she slid from bed and put out the kerosene heater. The wooden floorboards were icy against her bare feet. She gathered some clothes and the vinyl bag that held her toothbrush. Inserting her feet into furry pink slippers, she went into the corridor and headed for the bathroom at the end.

Although the house lacked electricity there was a limited supply of cold water to operate the plumbing. In the process of opening Haven for the seminar Hale and McNeil had filled a copper cistern in the attic of the east wing with water from an old dug well in the cellar. Everyone had been cautioned to use it sparingly and boil it before drinking. Unfortunately without power there was no way to operate the water heater, Eliza reflected. When she wanted a bath she would have to boil water on the kitchen stove and carry it up to a tub.

A round stained-glass window at the end of the corridor colored the slanting beams of the morning sun. On the right a narrow enclosed staircase led up to the third level. The two bathrooms were side by side on the left. Someone had used chalk to write "Boys" on one door and "Girls" on the other.

Footsteps pounded down the stair. She waited in the bathroom doorway. Mohan swung into view around the frame of the stairwell. The knees of his immaculately creased dress pants and the front of his sweater vest were smudged with dust.

"Eliza, you are a late sleeper. Everybody else is dressed and about long ago."

"Where are they all?"

"Everywhere." He waved his hand vaguely. "Can't stop to talk now. I'm helping Dr. Hale explore the house."

"Did you find anything interesting?"

"Yes. Something very, very important."

"What?"

"I cannot tell you." He put his finger to his smiling lips. "Dr. Hale has sworn me to secrecy."

Before she could question him further he hurried past her.

Shrugging, Eliza entered the bathroom and experimented with the decorative Victorian plumbing which the renovators apparently had not had the heart to replace, then washed herself in freezing water and dressed in the same drab brown sweater jacket and wool pants she had worn the previous day. She was not overly fond of these things, but the rest of her wardrobe was limited to a pair of corduroy slacks, a spare sweater and a few shirts.

Idly she wished it had been possible to pack more clothes. Hale's letter had specified only one suitcase. Everyone had complied with this sensible luggage limit except Amber, who had been unable to content herself with less than two large cases and a smaller carry-on bag.

She returned to her room and pulled on her high boots. From far parts of the house she heard murmurs of conversation. Her nose picked up the faint aroma of bacon.

She noticed that the door to Lee's room stood half open. No one was in the corridor. Furtively she pushed the door wider.

"Lee—?"

She had not expected an answer.

The room was similar to hers, but furnished by the capricious Hale with a narrow cot and a tall walnut wardrobe. The bed was made. A conservative brown leather suitcase sat upright in a corner. Nothing had been left lying about. There was a scent in the air which she tentatively identified as cologne.

Eliza crossed to the window and looked out. The room was on the north side and gave a magnificent view of the ocean and the beach. The weather had cleared completely. Snow covered the land in low drifts and frosted the grim black face of the ax-shaped point of rock on the far side of the inlet.

"I've discovered your secret vice—you're a snoop."

Eliza whirled around. Amber stood in the doorway, arms crossed and shoulder resting against the jamb. Coloring, Eliza went to her.

"I'm looking for Lee."

"Aren't we all."

The redhead turned and Eliza followed her into the passage, studying with suppressed envy the way her white turtleneck and skin-tight black leather pants enhanced her waist and hips. She noticed that Amber carried something in her hand.

"What's that?"

Amber held it up with a look of distaste.

"Charcoal from the fireplace. Messy stuff. I had some bad dreams last night. I'm going to seal my door."

She closed the door of her bedroom and began to draw a geometric design on the outer panel.

"Mind if I watch?" Eliza said.

"Why not? This is a New England hex sign. Guaranteed to frighten off goblins, spooks and other bump-in-the-nighters."

"What was it about?"

"Um?"

"Your dream."

Amber was silent a moment.

"I'd rather not talk about it."

Eliza did not press. She extended her awareness and felt a shiver of revulsion deep in the mind of the other woman. Surprisingly she found no animosity toward herself.

"Are you scanning me?" Amber asked without turning.

Eliza dropped her eyes.

"I have a certain sensitivity, you know," Amber said. "My magic may not be as flashy as Lee's but I get by."

Eliza watched the hex sign grow into a complex six-pointed star with curving lines around its center. It stood out strongly against the eggshell-colored paint on the door.

"You're not the only one who had a nightmare," she said with a shudder. "I dreamt about my mother. It was awful."

In a few words she recounted the events of her dream while Amber continued to sketch the hex sign.

"That's odd," Amber said, looking at her.

"What? That we both had nightmares?"

"More than that. My dream was about my step-father. He wasn't much of a father, if you know what I mean."

Eliza felt deep hurt beneath the bitterness in her voice. She put her hand on the shoulder of the other woman. Amber shook it off and returned to her drawing.

"Do you mind if I ask you something?" Eliza said.

"Shoot."

"Why did you come to Haven?"

"Why did you?" Amber shot back.

"I don't know. I thought I could help. It sounded interesting." She hesitated. "And I don't really have anywhere to go at Christmas."

"I came because I was bored to death," Amber said.

She set the charcoal on the floor and stepped back, dusting off her fingers.

"There. I'll sleep better tonight."

"Where is Lee anyway?"

"He and Allan went into the woods looking for a tree. This is Christmas Eve, remember, and boys will be boys."

"I hope they're safe."

Amber laughed.

"There's no danger. This whole field trip is one big fiasco."

"We don't know that yet. Mary—"

"Is a frustrated, hysterical girl looking for attention. She should be in therapy."

"Hale seems to think there's a threat," Eliza said defensively.

"Where? Since we've been here nothing has happened to any of us."

"What about our dreams?"

"Don't tell me you've never had a nightmare before," Amber mocked.

Eliza turned away to hide her irritation.

"I'm going to the kitchen to get something to eat."

"Liza?"

Eliza stopped.

"I know you're interested in Lee. I thought I should tell you that you're wasting your time—he doesn't like girls."

"What?" Eliza laughed.

"It's true," Amber continued seriously. "Last night I was feeling expansive after the scotch. I went to his room. I even climbed into bed with him. He sent me away."

Eliza was shocked by the casual way Amber admitted her actions, but did not allow her emotions to show.

"That doesn't prove anything. Did he tell you he was gay?"

"Not in so many words."

"I suppose it never occurred to you that he might be celibate?"

Amber blinked, then slowly smiled.

"No, it didn't. The poor dear. Maybe I can still help him."

I should have kept quiet, Eliza thought as she made her way down the main staircase. Amber would have left him alone. Now she'll be on him like a bitch in heat. Well, it's not my concern.

Mary greeted her in the kitchen and lifted a plate out of the warmer on the stove.

"I kept these hot for you. I knew you'd be hungry when you got up."

Eliza stared at the plate of fried eggs and bacon in delight.

"I thought I smelled bacon. But you shouldn't have bothered, Mary."

Mary brushed the admonition aside.

"The Professor and I had a talk, and he agreed to make me cook. I'm a farm girl and I know my way around a wood stove, which is a whole lot more than the rest of you can say. Anyway, I like to keep my hands busy."

"Well I'm sure you'll get no argument from the group," said Eliza past a folded section of bacon. "But I hope you didn't wash the dishes from last night. That was Amber's job."

"No, she did them," said Mary. She opened the stove door and shoved a section of maple log into the fire. "But to tell the truth, she did such a poor job that when she was finished I took them all out and did them again. Promise you won't let on?"

Amused, Eliza solemnly agreed not to inform Amber.

"I wouldn't expect this kind of breakfast from a nutritionist," she said as Mary poured her a glass of orange juice.

"Just because I've got to feed people tasteless, predigested pap when they're sick doesn't mean I've forgotten how to cook real food."

She poured herself a mug of steaming black coffee from the pot on the stove and sat down next to Eliza.

"How's your hand?" Eliza asked.

"Nearly better." Mary showed her the ugly red sear along her palm. "It wasn't a bad burn. Just needed a little butter."

"You really frightened us last night when you went into your trance. Is that the right word, trance?"

Mary blushed.

"I just call it makin' out pictures. I didn't mean to scare nobody."

"We were scared for you," Eliza said.

"You don't need to be scared for me. I've been makin' out pictures since I was five. It doesn't cause any harm."

"Does it always happen like that?"

Mary sipped her coffee and shook her head.

"No, last night was real sudden. Usually I can control it."

She frowned to herself.

"When I was little I used to scare people. They said I was the Devil's child. My daddy whipped me to make me stop, until I got so that I could control it most times. But every now and then it just happens."

"Mary, did you dream last night?"

"Indeed I did. I dreamed I was a little girl back on the farm in Arkansas waitin' for my daddy to give me a whipping. He always used to whip us kids on the back porch. It was so real it almost scared the pee out of me. But it wasn't daddy who came, it was a big shadow with burning eyes."

She shivered and cupped the mug of steaming coffee with both hands as she drank.

It's too much of a coincidence, Eliza thought. All three of us have nightmares, and all three concern unhappy memories of our childhood. But what connection can it possibly have with Haven?

Her reverie was broken by the entrance of Mohan, who looked around the kitchen with disappointment.

"Do not tell me that Lee and Allan have yet to return?"

"They're still outside," Mary said.

He shook his head and sighed.

"This is very bad. Dr. Hale wishes to see everyone in the gathering room at once. He has an important discovery he wishes to reveal."

"He'll just have to wait," Mary said pleasantly. "Sit down and have some coffee, Mohan."

"No, I must go out and look for them. Dr. Hale will be angry."

He took his scarf from the coat rack behind the door and began to anxiously loop it around his neck. Mary got up and forcibly guided him over to the table.

"For heaven sake, will you sit down and relax. Much as I respect the Professor, he's not God Almighty. The boys will come in when they're ready."

Mohan started to protest. Eliza got up and took her own coat and beret down from the rack.

"I'll go. I need the fresh air anyway."

"Thank you, Eliza, that is very good of you," Mohan said sincerely.

"You know what your trouble is, Mohan? You fuss too much," Mary told him. "Sometimes you just have to let a log find its own way down the river."

Eliza opened the door and stepped into the much cooler air of the back hall. A sudden thought made her stop and turn.

"Mohan, did you have any dreams last night?"

"I never dream," he said, watching Mary pour his coffee. "Why do you ask?"

"It doesn't matter."

Eliza felt strong disappointment. That was the end of her lovely dream pattern. Maybe it had been only coincidence after all.

"You be careful in those woods," Mary said suddenly.

"You're as bad as Mohan," Eliza told her irritably. "There's nothing out there. According to Amber this whole seminar is a waste of time."

"She's dead wrong," Mary said with conviction. She gazed out the windows at the distant trees. "There's danger, I can feel it. Someone is walking under the shadow of death."

"If you feel that way, why don't you ask Hale to use the radio to call the boat?"

"That wouldn't be right," she said, shaking her head sadly. "I gave my word that I would see this through to the end and I mean to do it."

She went to the doorway and took Eliza by her shoulders.

"But you mind what I tell you. Something in this house is watching us, and its thoughts are not kindly. It's all twisted up and bitter inside. It means to make us suffer. Then it means to kill us, one by one."

# 6

It was cold in the shadow of Haven. The white cloud of Eliza's breath hung around her shoulders like wisps of cotton wool before dispersing. She paused on the back step for several seconds, drawing in deep lungfuls of crisp air heavily laden with the scent of evergreen and the salt tang of the sea. There was a glorious freshness in everything that intoxicated her senses. It was such a relief to escape the oppressive gloom of the house.

If I were looking for a Christmas tree, which way would I go? she wondered. Two lines of footprints led across the drifts on the back lawn into the woods. Eliza set out to follow them.

As she stepped into the sunlight a flicker of movement drew her attention to a low building lying close under the edge of the trees. It was almost as if someone had ducked behind its corner.

Lee?" she called uncertainly. "Is that you?"

The out building stood facing the house. It was a large solid structure with heavy beam fram-

ing and a green copper roof. Eliza realized suddenly that it must be the stable where the horses
had died.

The silence made her nervous. She extended
her mind and felt a mischievous presence waiting
behind the corner of the building. The emotion was
quite faint, as though veiled by some barrier.
Amber's words about boys being boys came back
to her.

Collecting her courage, she forced herself on
stiff legs toward the stable.

"You might as well come out. I know you're
there."

I won't give them the satisfaction of scaring
me, she thought. As she rounded the back corner
she tightened her hands into fists inside her mittens
to prepare herself.

Nobody jumped out. The back side of the
building was deserted. Puzzled, Eliza continued to
walk all around the structure, trying the locked
double doors as she passed. Plywood sheets pre-
vented her from seeing in the windows.

The distant murmur of conversation in the
woods made her shelve the mystery for later con-
sideration. She set off toward the voices at a quick
pace before Lee and Allan wandered out of hearing. Here the ground was relatively flat and open.
Walking was easy except where her path inter-
sected the crests of the low drifts, which rose no
higher than her shins. Golden sunlight slanted
through bare boughs of mature birch and maple.
Eliza guessed that at one time this part of the

woods had been cleared, since the evergreens had not yet regained full control.

So peaceful, she thought. So safe. The woods and gently rising hills seemed to cherish and protect her. It was years since she had walked alone under the trees. Not since that final summer in the family cottage on the lake, the year of her father's death. It had been the last truly happy year of her life. Her mother never recovered from the shock.

Care of her mother, the pressures of the funeral, the settlement of the estate, and then later committing her mother to the institution—all these burdens had fallen upon her immature shoulders like a yoke of servitude. Only the word used by her aunts and uncles was duty. Servitude. Duty. It amounted to the same thing, in the end.

She stumbled and caught herself on the ice-crusted bough of a small spruce. The jolt brought her mind back to the present. She saw that in front of her the ground dropped away into a shallow irregular bowl cut in the base of a low cliff. Broken blocks of stone lay scattered about everywhere, their jagged edges frosted with snow. It was a dangerous place to walk without looking. Stepping into the depression, Eliza picked her way with care across the loose rocks to its center.

The pit was not a natural formation. Some of the rocks had round holes drilled in them, and there were signs of tool marks on others. She realized this must be the quarry the original builders of Haven had used to get stone for the foundation. That was why a broad track had been cleared

through the forest. The masons had needed a
wagon to move the cut stone to the building site.

Eliza picked up a stone chip and tossed it
across the pit. It clattered over the rocks with a dry
echo and vanished noiselessly under the snow.
There was a feeling of abandonment about the
place, almost of desolation. Piles of stones still
waited for the wagon that would bear them away.
They had rested there for over a century and would
remain unmoved, for all she know, until the end of
the world.

A shadow passed over her face. She looked
up at the sun, expecting to see the silhouette of a
soaring eagle. The sky was empty. With a shiver
she realized she had spent more time investigating
the quarry than she had intended. She listened
intently. The murmur of voices no longer reached
her through the trees.

Lee and Allan are probably back at Haven by
now, she thought. Suddenly the notion of searching
for them deeper into the woods was not appealing.
She turned around with a prickling on the back of
her neck. Even though she told herself she was
being foolish the sensation would not go away. The
naked rock face of the cliff frowned at her in disap-
proval. Drawing her fur collar tight around her
throat, she climbed out of the quarry and retraced
her footprints between the trees.

The prints of her boots undulated through the
drifts between the stark, frozen trunks of the trees
until they blended into the gloom of the forest.
Viewed in the distance they might almost be mis-

taken for the tracks of some large animal. It was easier to walk in the hollows then beside them. The sun made the snow slippery. Eliza picked her steps with care to keep from falling.

Abruptly she froze motionless, heart pounding in terror. She bent slowly forward and studied the marks in front of her, then straightened with a jerk and turned a complete circle, staring wide-eyed all about at the breathless trees. Lifting her boot, she pressed it into the snow beside one of the prints and gently removed it. For several seconds she regarded the two impressions in disbelief. Her reason fought a brief battle with her senses and lost. It was impossible. But there was no doubt. These were not her own tracks that she followed.

The line of prints curved gently, almost imperceptibly, leading her away from Haven and deeper into the woods. Had she continued to follow them she would certainly have become lost. She remembered the mischievous presence behind the stable, and the shadow at the quarry. The conviction grew that something was stalking her, playing a malicious game with her, a game with deadly consequences.

From where the track vanished among the trees she heard the murmur of voices. Ignoring the sound, Eliza took a bearing from the sun and set out across the unbroken snow in the direction where she knew Haven must lie. It required all of her inner resolve to keep a walking pace and not break into panic flight.

The inviting air of the woods had been only a ploy designed to lure her away from safety. She sensed a hostile presence following close behind, waiting for her to slip and fall. But when she turned to look there was nothing. Something dry rustled at her heels. Eliza broke into a floundering, sliding run, then with agonizing effort forced herself to slow her steps. If she ran she was lost. Primal instinct warned her the watcher would fasten upon her fear and use it to destroy her.

A line of prints appeared in the virgin snow ahead. For a moment she experienced the horrifying suspicion that she had walked in a circle. Then she realized she had regained her original track, which meant she was headed in the right direction. Her disordered mind seized on the familiar impressions in the snow the way a drowning victim grasps a lifeline. She followed them heel to toe, at every anxious step expecting to be seized from behind by some malicious potency.

With startling abruptness she emerged onto the frozen back lawn of Haven. Lee and Allan were just coming out of the trees a hundred yards or so to her right. In the distance the slender body of the theurgist looked almost feminine, an illusion heightened by the tapered waist of his navy pea jacket. Lee dragged a bushy evergreen behind him by its stump. He saw her and waved with the axe he carried in his other hand.

She waved back and turned apprehensively. Once more the woods appeared quiet, serene and inviting. The terror that had gripped her heart in its icy fist only moments before had melted away like a forgotten dream. Forcing down a shudder, she ran to the men.

"Ugg, we great hunters," Allan said. He put a hand behind his head and stuck up two fingers. "We bring heap much tree-meat for white squaw to cook."

"Chauvinist," said Eliza, eyeing him. He seemed overly animated, but perhaps it was only an illusion caused by her strained senses.

"Where were you?" Lee asked.

She evaded his eyes.

"Exploring. I found the stone quarry where the foundation of Haven was mined."

"Are you all right?"

"Sure."

She needed time to collect herself before telling him of the footprints. After what Amber had said about Mary, she did not want to seem hysterical.

Lee said nothing. Eliza knew he was dissatisfied with her response. He senses things, she thought, or reads them in my face.

They dragged the tree into the gathering room and cleared a corner. It was a pine, perfect except for a double crown and one missing bough near the bottom. Mary dug up an old galvanized bucket, and Allan with the help of Lee managed to wedge the tree upright in it with several bricks. They filled the bucket with water and dropped in two aspirin from the first-aid kit.

"There are no decorations," Amber said, looking at the evergreen critically with folded arms. "And it's crooked."

"We'll have to decorate it the old-fashion way and make our own," said Mary.

Mohan and Hale entered the room crabwise, bent double under the weight of a large wooden trunk. Luther trotted in behind them and claimed the hearth. They let the trunk drop with a bang. Hale took out a handkerchief and wiped his glistening face. He had stripped off his sweater and rolled up the sleeves of his blue flannelette shirt.

"With all the racket you were making down here I'd thought you'd scared up the Devil himself," he said, staring at the tree.

"Not perfectly perpendicular," Allan said with a glance at Amber. "But what's Christmas without a tree?"

"What's Christmas anyway, but a pagan festival stolen by the Church for its own purposes?" she retorted.

"Amber is quite right," Hale said. "Originally Christmas was a pagan celebration designed to lure the sun back from the depths of midwinter. The tree itself is a pagan symbol, not Christian."

"However it started, that's not to say it isn't Christian nowadays," Mary said somewhat indignantly.

"Of course," said Hale. "You're right, Mary. Festivals change and grow just like everything else."

"What have you and Mohan found in the attic?" Lee asked, eyeing the trunk.

"Something rich and strange," said Hale with a smile. "Something that may throw light on the unwritten history of Haven."

"What are we waiting for?" Allan said. "Let's open it."

Eliza gathered her resolve and stepped in front of the trunk.

"Before you do that I need to tell you what happened while I was in the woods."

They looked at her curiously.

"Did you see something?" Lee asked.

"Yes. In a way."

"Go ahead, Eliza," Hale encouraged. "We need phenomena to work on or we won't have a seminar."

"Some of you may think I'm being hysterical," she said, glancing at Amber.

In a few unemotional words she told of finding the strange footprints, and described her uncontrollable panic. She left out the shadow by the stable and the voices in the woods. Both could be explained away by natural events such as snow dropping from the roof of the stable or wind among the trees. Even though she knew these explanations were insufficient she had no proof, and did not wish her whole story to be dismissed as an hallucination induced by fear.

"You say the terror left you the moment you stepped out of the woods?" Lee inquired gently.

Eliza nodded.

"That suggests your fear was artificially induced."

"Is that important?"

"It would mean that whatever we're facing has the power to manipulate our emotions," Hale explained.

"That might account for some of the deaths at Haven," Amber put in. "Suicides resulting from induced depression."

"Possibly," Hale said. "However I'm convinced that some of the phenomena are physical."

He sat on the domed lid of the trunk and crossed a leg over a knee. He tugged his beard meditatively.

"The prints you saw must belong to one of us. Who was in the woods today?"

"Only Lee and Allan," said Amber. "Apart from Eliza, that is."

The tracks weren't made by any of us. They were too small," Eliza said.

"Luther, then," suggested Hale. "I let him out this morning."

"They were too large for a dog. Anyway, they were human."

Eliza felt herself being put subtly on the defensive. They think I imagined everything, she realized. Resentment began to swell inside of her. She looked around for support. Lee's eyes held sympathy. Mary was looking at the floor. Eliza felt her cheeks begin to burn.

"Maybe they were the tracks of a moose, or a bear," Allan said.

"No, they were made by human feet." She had to fight to keep shrillness out of her voice.

"How can you be so positive?" Amber asked skeptically.

Eliza glared at them.

"Because I saw the outline of toes, damn it! They were a child's footprints—a barefoot child!"

**7**

They stared at her in silence.

"I know it sounds crazy, but I'm certain of what I saw. Look for yourselves if you don't believe me."

"We believe you, Eliza," Hale said gently. "But I do want to get verification. This is our first physical manifestation. I wish you'd told me immediately. It shouldn't be hard to find the tracks. Will someone volunteer to go photograph and measure them?"

"I'll go," Allan said. "Anything to get out of this tomb."

"All right, but take Mohan with you. I don't want anyone alone where it can be avoided. We need verification of all incidents."

Allan picked up the adjustable Polaroid camera that was part of Hale's field equipment and left with Mohan.

Hale dragged the trunk beside the conference table and busied himself opening its ornamental iron catches.

"I'll show you what we found in the attic. I imagine Mohan will fill Allan in as they walk."

Mary put her heavy hand on Eliza's shoulder and drew her aside.

"Did you feel anything near you in the woods?" she asked seriously.

"I got the sense of being watched, but it may have been only imagination."

"This morning I thought I felt a presence in the house," Mary said. "It's real slippery, though. I can't quite make it out."

Hale raised his head from the trunk at her words but said nothing. He glanced significantly at Lee and Amber.

"The worst part," Eliza said with a shudder, "Was that the footprints led all the way up to the quarry. It must have been standing right behind me."

At Hale's direction they gathered around the conference table. Amber, Mary and Eliza sat with their backs to the windows. Lee sat on the opposite side next to Hale, who pulled a bundle from the trunk and unrolled it across the tabletop. It was a garment of some kind, Eliza saw, a long and heavy robe.

"What do you make of this, Lee?" Hale said.

Lee gently spread the robe apart. It clung to itself with gray-green mildew and exhaled a musty odor.

"Ceremonial dress of some kind."

"Familiar to you?"

"No."

"Satanic?"

He brushed the dust off an embroidered emblem on the left breast of the garment.

"I doubt it. This cloth is dark blue—almost a purple. Satanists normally use red or black robes. And this emblem is a variation on the rose-cross. See, a flaming heart over a gold cross on a silver field."

"Not a white lodge, though."

"No—more like a gray, if there is such a thing."

"Would you two mind telling me what you're talking about?" Amber broke in.

Hale gestured to the trunk on the floor beside him.

"This is the trunk of a ceremonial magician. His ritual robe you see on the table." He reached down and began taking things out of the chest. "This is his cap. His circlet. His sash. His shoes. His lamen. And his rod."

The last object he picked up gingerly with his fingertips and held it away from his body. It was a plain black wooden rod with caps of gold on each end.

"This gave me a nasty electrical shock when I touched it in the attic, but it isn't hurting me now. I seem to have earthed it."

He passed the rod around the table. Eliza was surprised at how heavy it felt. It must be made out of solid ebony, she thought. There was a clinging aura of corrupt potency about it. Mary refused even to touch the rod, and drew back when it was passed to Amber. The witch twirled it between her fingers like a baton, then gave it to Lee.

"There's some writing on the lamen," Hale said. "For those who don't know, a lamen is a personal emblem of power used to project authority over spirits."

Lee picked up the large silver medallion by its chain from the table. It turned slowly in the chill northern window light. Heavy gold wire inlaid across its tarnished face formed an interlocking star with eight points. Strange signs and marks like letters adorned its back.

"This looks like Enochian script," he said.

"So it is, along with some Hebrew and Arabic names of spirits. But it's the three Enochian letters in the center that interest me."

Taking the lamen, Hale went to the small green chalkboard he had erected on an artist's easel and copied the marks from right to left:

$$\mathtt{I} \, \cap \, \vee$$

"D, P, B," Lee translated. "Daniel P. Brannon?"

Hale's gray eyes fairly danced with glee.

"So it would seem!"

"Brannon, a magician?" Eliza said. "You told us he was an industrialist."

"And a speculator, and an architect, and a philanthropist. But most of all, a mystery," Hale said.

"It looks like gibberish," said Amber, eyeing the chalk marks.

"Enochian is an inspired language believed by some to be the original tongue of the angelic hierarchy," Hale said.

"It was supernaturally revealed to the Eliza-
bethan philosopher John Dee around the end of the
sixteenth century," Lee added meditatively as he
fingered the rod.

Leaning over the table, Hale extended the
lamen to Mary.

"I want you to read this, Mary. Will you do
that?"

"Of course, Professor," Mary said, sinking
weakly in her chair. "That's why I'm here, isn't it."

With unwilling fingers she accepted the
blackened disk and cupped it between her hands.
Her eyes closed. Eliza reached out to her and felt a
dark gulf open in the mind of the other woman.

"What do you see, Mary?" Hale prompted.

"A face." Dread dulled her voice.

"Describe it."

"Strong. Old. Cruel mouth and sharp eyes."

"Is it the face of the portrait in the front hall?"

"Yes—it's hard to tell—I think so."

"That's because she's seeing his magical image
along with his physical features," Lee murmured.

Looking past Mary's strained profile, Eliza
was surprised by the genuine concern in Amber's
green eyes. For the first time she realized that
Amber's cynical veneer was only a mask to hide
her deeper feelings. Amber felt her gaze and sat
back in her chair.

"Can you make out any surroundings,
Mary?" said Hale. "Try to expand your vision."

"It's dark." Mary's voice became distant. "I
see candles. Men standing inside circles. There's a

big triangle on the floor and three smaller circles where men stand looking out at the darkness. There's something in the triangle."

"What? What's in the triangle?"

"It's like smoke. No, more like a shadow. And it's moving—swirling—it's dancing around and around. The air is rushing and blowing the hair and the robes of the men. There's a roar like the waves of the sea. It's so big—bright and dark at the same time. Like a big dancing flame—oh!"

She opened her eyes and let the lamen clatter onto the table.

"I'm sorry," she said. "I didn't want to drop it, but it suddenly felt hot."

Amber put out her hand to pick it up and drew back.

"Mary didn't imagine that. Put your hand over it, Lee."

Lee held his palm a few inches over the surface of the lamen. He gradually lowered it and touched the silver disk gingerly several times.

"It's warm," he said. "But it's cooling rapidly."

He picked the lamen up and juggled it like a baked potato. Where it had lain on the table a singed ring showed in the varnished board.

"Are you burned, Mary?" Hale asked.

Mary held up her fingers. They were unmarked.

"I let go the moment I felt it."

"There's a power here," said Hale. "And it obviously doesn't want us poking into its past."

He went to the rolltop desk and brought back his compact video camera and a battery-powered portable television with a flat folding color screen about the size of a paperback.

This is the tape of an interview I conducted last March with George Three-Rivers, a Micmac Indian living on the Eskasoni Reservation in East Bay, Cape Breton," he murmured, connecting the camera to the television with a video jack. "Three-Rivers was a handyman at Haven while it was owned by Biddingford from 1911 to 1943. He even claims to remember Brannon. I'm afraid the sound quality is poor. Please listen carefully."

He positioned the television at the end of the table so that everyone could see it and set the camera to play the pre-recorded video tape onto the screen. The picture flickered, then stabilized to show the shriveled face of a very old man propped up in a steel bed frame with two pillows behind his back. His long snow-white hair lay like a cloud over his shoulders. Faded roses covered the paper on the wall behind the bed.

"Mr. Three-Rivers?" Hale's voice came from somewhere off camera. "You were telling me about Haven."

"I remember." The voice of the Indian was no more than a husky whisper. He spoke with a flat but indefinable accent. "What do you want to know?"

"The night of the fire—the fire that gutted the west wing—were you working?"

"It was my night off, but one of the waiters got sick, so they asked me to fill in. I was a good-looking man in those days."

He smiled at the memory, then abruptly started to cough. Rolling out of the camera frame to the side of the bed, he spat up phlegm and lay weakly back on the pillows.

"Were you in the hall when the fire started?"

"No. I was in the kitchen."

"What did you do?"

"We heard all the yelling and screaming and I run along with the rest of them to look. We pushed open the big double doors on the ballroom."

His eyes widened and he fell silent.

"What did you see?" Hale prompted.

"The tree that stood in the middle of the room—it was on its side blazing like a pine torch, the flames licking right up to the ceiling and showers of sparks falling on the ladies' long dresses. They were all running around knocking into things and screaming. I guess they were crazy with fear."

"So it was the blue spruce getting knocked into the fireplace that started it."

The Indian shook his head.

"I read that story in the newspaper but that was wrong."

"How do you mean?"

"That tree was nowhere near the fireplace."

"Are you sure? You said yourself the air was filled with smoke."

"I didn't need more than one look. The fireplace is in the south wall. That tree fell north toward the windows."

"Do you know how it got knocked over?"

The old man shook his head and closed his eyes. After a few moments his breaths deepened. It was evident that he had drifted into sleep.

Hale shut off the play-back on the camera.

"This bit coming up concerns the phenomena that occurred in the months prior to the fire. Three-Rivers was the only living witness to these events."

"Was?" inquired Amber.

"Shortly after this series of interviews he fell asleep with a cigarette in his hand and burned to death in his bed."

"The poor man," Mary said.

Hale turned the camera back on. The television showed Three-Rivers sitting up in a wooden armchair with a blanket wrapped around his shoulders. The wall behind him was shingled. Sunlight fell across his hollow cheek. A cigarette dangled from the corner of his mouth.

"This was recorded on the back porch of the house owned by Three-Rivers' daughter, who was taking care of him," Hale explained as his own voice spoke from the television.

"Mr. Three-Rivers, you told me yesterday funny things were going on at Haven in the year of the fire."

"That's right." The voice of the Indian was stronger than in the previous segment.

"Did you see any of these things yourself?"

"All the time. You couldn't turn around that autumn without something strange happening. I was ready to quit."

"Tell me some things that happened to you."

"Voices in empty rooms. Children laughing when nobody was there. Doors opening and slamming shut by themselves."

"You actually heard and saw these things?"

"Hell, we all did."

"Why didn't you tell someone?"

"Everyone knew what was going on."

"I mean someone outside, like a newspaper."

"Mr. Biddingford warned us not to. He would have fired me. I needed that job."

"Then Biddingford himself knew about the incidents."

The Indian laughed silently, took the cigarette from his mouth and spat to the side of the chair.

"He knew. He had to send his wife away on account of it."

"How was that?"

"One night she ran stark naked out into the snow. She claimed something tried to drown her while she was taking a bath."

"Did she say what it looked like, this thing?"

"Not to me, but I heard the story. She called it a tall shadow with glittering eyes and flaming hair—those were her own words."

"How long before the fire was this?"

Three-Rivers looked meditatively into the distance.

"About a week or so."

"Can you think back to when the trouble first started?"

"I know exactly when it started."

"You do?"

"It was when Biddingford opened that sealed room."

There was a pause, then a rustle of movement from somewhere off camera. When Hale's voice came it was tense with suppressed excitement.

"Would you tell me about the room, Mr. Three-Rivers? Please think very carefully, it may be important."

The Indian drew on his cigarette and let the smoke out slowly.

"It happened about the beginning of April in forty-three. Mr. Biddingford decided to make some improvements in the plumbing. It was the off-season—not much business anyway because of the war in Europe. While he was going over the plans of the hotel he spotted a room that no one had ever seen. He got real interested and made a bunch of us help him search for it."

"Where was this room located?"

"On the third floor—we called it the attic—just above the front hall."

"And this room was deliberately hidden?"

"Somebody built a wall right over it. We chipped off the plaster and lath and there was this door underneath with some fancy design painted on it."

"Do you remember the design?"

"No, it's been too many years. I don't recall it."

"Who opened the door?"

"Biddingford. It was locked shut and didn't have no knob, so he grabbed a wrecking bar out of my hand and pried it open. He was like a crazy man. I think he somehow got the idea there was money hid in that room."

"Was there?"

"Hell no. It was empty."

"And that's when funny things started to happen?"

"Right then. When Biddingford opened the door a gust of wind blew out that damn near knocked him over. The air smelled real bad. Like death."

"Do you remember what the room looked like?"

"Damnedest place you ever saw. Painted flat black from top to bottom. Even the floor. And there weren't no windows or lights."

"What did Biddingford do when he found it empty?"

"He was disappointed pretty bad. He had the door to the room boarded over. Said it wasn't good for nothing the way it was, and it wasn't worth the trouble to fix it."

Once more Hale stopped the camera and regarded his listeners intently.

"This last bit was something I got early in my first conversation with Three-Rivers. It didn't strike me as important at the time."

He started the camera. Once again the scene showed the old man propped up in his bed.

"You said your father worked for Daniel Brannon, the builder of Haven By the Sea?"

"For twenty-three years."

"Did you ever see Brannon yourself?"

"A few times. I was just a kid. No more than seven or eight years old."

"What was he like?"

"He was a big, stern man. Used to scare me silly when he looked at me. He was always holding conferences with men who came to Haven from foreign countries. They spoke French and German and a bunch of other languages I didn't recognize."

"Do you remember who any of the men were?"

"No. I do recall one funny thing, now that I think back on it."

"About the men who came to see Brannon?"

"It was the way they shook hands. I remember hiding behind the door and watching them."

"I don't understand. How did they shake hands?"

"It was different from regular people. I can't describe it. Give my your hand."

Hale leaned into view on the television screen from the left and allowed Three-Rivers to take his hand.

"It was like this, with the two thumbs together. Feels funny, doesn't it?"

Hale shut off the camera and rewound the video cassette.

"Some kind of Masonic sign?" Lee suggested.

"I've seen handshakes similar to it, but not the same," Hale said. "Here, give me your hand."

Lee extended his hand and Hale shook it, showing them the way the thumbs came together.

"I don't see where this is leading us," Amber

said suddenly. "Suppose Brannon was a magician. Suppose he belonged to some bizarre Masonic order. Brannon died in 1911. The phenomena didn't begin until 1943. How do you explain the lapse of those thirty-two years?"

"The black room. It's that, isn't it?" said Mary with hushed conviction.

"I think so, yes," Hale agreed. "I'm not sure how or why, but Brannon must have sealed something into that room before his death. When Biddingford opened the door he released it. It's been free ever since, haunting this house."

This was what Hale had been holding back the previous day, Eliza realized. He had known about the black chamber all along, but had not mentioned it for fear of frightening them off. She wondered what other horrible secrets he was hiding. Did he know something about the watcher in the woods? Was he really cold-blooded enough to place them all at risk just to insure their cooperation? Suddenly she wished she had taken the opportunity to leave with McNeil in the boat.

# 8

While Eliza was considering whether on not to confront Hale over the devious way he had withheld the full truth about Haven, Allan and Mohan came bustling in, their cheeks still red with cold. Allan dropped the Polaroid on the desk and handed Hale a set of pictures.

"Not too good, I'm afraid," he said. "We found the tracks, but the sun must have deformed their outline."

Hale tossed the photographs on the table.

"Not good at all. This is the kind of evidence skeptics love to ridicule."

Eliza picked up several of the snaps. One was a distant shot showing a line of footprints in the snow. The others were close-ups of several individual prints with a measuring tape beside them. They were merely depressions in the snow without detail. They might have been anything.

"They were clearer when I saw them," she said.

"I'm sure, but that doesn't help us any now, does it," Hale said, struggling with his frustration.

Allan picked up the lamen and rod and examined them.

"Interesting. Mohan's been telling me about your chest. Is it Brannon's magical box?"

"So it appears. I want you to watch this video. I've just played it for the rest, but it's worth seeing twice."

They sat in silence while the tape played to the end uninterrupted. Then they discussed the theory of the black room.

"There are ways of binding a hostile entity," Allan said. "But usually it's easier just to send it away."

"Maybe Brannon wasn't strong enough to banish it," Eliza suggested. "He was old."

"Or perhaps he did not wish to," said Mohan.

"We'll never find out this way." Hale stood decisively. "Mohan and I have located the entrance to the black room. I propose that we open and enter it. Any objections?"

No one spoke.

"Fair enough. Let's get to work."

As they moved through the front hall Eliza noticed Allan lagging behind. She watched him from the corner of her eye and saw him slip aside into the entrance to the rear corridor. The others, who were listening to Hale as they followed him up the staircase, had their attention directed forward. Quietly Eliza backed down the stairs and went after the theurgist.

He stood just out of sight around the edge of the passage door. She watched him tip from a small vial into his palm two brightly-colored pills. Lifting his hand to his mouth, he leaned back his head and closed his eyes as he swallowed them.

"Allan, are you sick?"

He jumped and stared at her, then grinned crookedly.

"No, but these are good for what ails you. Care to try one?"

She waved aside the proffered vial. Capping it, he put it into the pocket of his jeans.

"We can't keep secrets from you, can we, Eliza? I expect that's why Hale asked you along."

"I noticed you were acting differently from yesterday, but I never suspected drugs."

He pushed himself away from the wall with his shoulder.

"The kind of magic I work requires large amounts of animal energy. It's not uncommon for goetic magicians to take stimulants."

"What were those pills—some kind of upper?"

"More or less."

They began to walk slowly toward the stairs after the rest of the group.

"Have you taken others?"

"Mescaline, cocaine, heroine, LSD—should I go on?"

"But why?" she asked angrily. "You don't need them."

"How could I know that until I tried them?"

"You're killing yourself."

He looked at her quizzically, as though wondering how to answer.

He thinks I'm a prude, Eliza thought. But he doesn't want to injure my feelings.

"The acknowledged span of a man's existence is three score and ten," he said. "Drugs may cut twenty years off my life. The way I see it, that leaves me with about thirty more good years."

"Not if you injure your mind."

He shrugged his thin shoulders.

"I'm already half mad. When I go over the edge it will be a relief."

She took him by the sleeve of his sweater and stopped him at the foot of the stairs.

"That's why you came to Haven, isn't it?"

"What do you mean?"

"You want to see how close to the edge you can push yourself."

A wild light danced in his dark eyes and he smiled in self-mockery.

"I need to grasp the beast by its throat and bare its face to the sun."

"I don't understand."

"Neither do I."

"Maybe if you talked to Lee—"

He shook his head.

"Lee is a good man. Straight as a die. When he says something you never have to wonder what he's thinking. But this is a matter I have to deal with alone."

"Does Professor Hale know?"

"He probably suspects, but we haven't discussed it."

They ascended the sweeping marble staircase in silence.

"I'd rather you didn't tell Hale," Allan said as they reached the landing. "It might precipitate an unnecessary confrontation."

Eliza felt the hard edge of arrogance and determination behind his words and knew it would be futile to inform Hale.

"All right." She touched his arm. "Allan, please be careful."

He smiled and patted her hand.

"Come on, you two," Amber called impatiently from the end of the east wing. "You're holding up the show."

Quickening their pace, they followed her down the length of the corridor and climbed the steep staircase to the third level. It was the first time Eliza had seen it. On either side of a dark, narrow central hallway were small rooms with sloped ceilings and dormer windows. Eliza glanced into the first room on the left. It contained Hale's battery-powered short-wave radio, positioned on a small table under the window. Apart from a single wooden chair and the table, the floor was empty.

They made their way back toward the center of the house where the others stood listening to Hale.

"This level was used in Biddingford's time to board the staff, and even an occasional guest when the hotel was pressed for space. Before that I'm not

sure what purpose these rooms served. The old servant quarters are in the other wing. The central
portion of this level contains several windowless
rooms that were evidently used for storage."

He led the group into the shadowy end of the
passage, which branched into a number of storage
rooms piled high with damaged and worn furniture and other junk.

"Because of the high cost of transportation,
everything not in use was either stored or burned,"
Hale commented.

The refuse of half a century seemed to be col-
lected together in these dark rooms. Eliza peered
uncertainly through the open doorways at the
gloomy interiors while Hale busied himself lighting a kerosene lamp. Mohan was occupied with the
video camera. Hale wanted the opening of the
black room preserved on tape.

"Look, a Victorian ball gown," Amber said
with delight.

She stepped into one of the rooms and began
to beat the dust off a yellowed satin gown hanging
from a wooden rack. The smell of age enveloped
them.

"It's Edwardian," said Allan, following her.

"So who asked you?" Amber retorted. "I
wonder if it would fit me?"

She pulled out the sleeve to measure against
her arm and the rotten stitches parted, leaving a
gaping hole. Disappointed, she let the fabric fall.

"This side, people." The voice of Professor Hale
drifted in to them. "The black room is on the north."

They wandered back into the passage. Eliza noticed Mary in one of the doorways looking with an odd intensity at the jumbled contents of the room beyond. She scanned the emotions of the other woman and was relieved to find no apprehension.

"What are you looking at?" she asked.

Mary gestured into the storeroom.

"Am I imagining things, Eliza, or is that furniture smaller than it ought to be? Look at that little chair."

Eliza looked over her shoulder at the furniture stacked nearest the door. There were numerous chairs visible, several bed frames, and a table lying on its side. The furniture did seem too small to be of practical use.

"Maybe it's doll furniture. Or maybe it was intended for children."

"I'll bet that's the answer," Mary said. "There must have been a nursery where the guests could leave their kids when they went off hunting and sailing."

She stepped into the room and laid her hand on one of the stacked chairs.

"It's so cute—" Her face became gray and vacant. She snatched her hand away.

"Mary, what's wrong?"

Eliza grabbed the other woman to keep her from falling.

"I'll be all right," she said weakly. "I wasn't ready for it, is all. Let me catch my breath."

"What's going on?" Hale entered the room, followed by Lee and Mohan.

Eliza described the incident.

"There was a sickness in the chair," Mary told him. "Sickness and death. I wasn't expecting it—not in a chair made for children."

"Do you want to go downstairs?"

"Goodness, no, leave me be. I'm fine."

Mohan and Hale helped her out of the room over her flustered protests. Lee remained beside Eliza. They were momentarily alone. Eliza fingered a broad strap that hung from an upturned bed frame, her back to him.

"I noticed this miniature furniture myself," Lee said. "Strange."

"What is?"

"I can't understand where it came from. No Edwardian resort hotel would cater to the whims of children by providing them with special furniture. In those days children were expected to mould themselves into the adult world."

"The furniture must have come from the time when Haven was still a private home," she suggested.

"That's even less likely. Brannon only had one son. There's enough furniture here for a dozen children."

They followed the reverberating voice of Hale to a larger room with some empty floor space. It was also windowless. The kerosene lamp on a table cast a pale yellow glow.

"Don't worry about the camera," Hale said to Mohan as they entered. "It adapts itself to low light."

He turned to Lee and Eliza, his ruddy face shining with enthusiasm.

"Mohan and I spent the entire morning clearing the junk away from this wall. It's a good thing George Three-Rivers was explicit in his directions or I might never have found the entrance to the black room, even knowing of its existence. It was completely hidden."

He picked up a crowbar and began to pry at one of a series of wide boards nailed from floor to ceiling horizontally across the wall. The rusty nails shrieked as they broke loose and began to pull out. Mohan crouched and moved around to get the best angle for the camera.

"I must be standing exactly where Biddingford stood on that fateful day in April long ago when in a frenzy of greed he pried at the door that lies concealed behind these planks," he said into the lens.

The board came loose and fell with a resonate clatter to the floor. Lee cleared it away from Hale's feet. It was at least sixteen inches wide, cut from the tree of a bygone era.

"I see something," Allan said.

He picked up the lamp and brought it closer. Through the gap in the boards a door was visible. Its jamb showed gouge marks and ragged splinters. An intricate geometric pattern of painted black and silver lines about the size of a human face adorned its surface. The design had a vaguely sinister appearance. It reminded Eliza of a black spider sitting in the center of a silver web, although it was too

abstract to actually depict anything. Peering at it
over Allan's shoulder, she found herself shivering.

"Stand back," Hale said, wiping sweat from
his forehead with the back of his wrist.

He attacked the remaining boards through
the opening and in a few minutes cleared the door.
Apart from the symbol, its panels were unpainted.
It lacked a latch or knob of any kind.

"We may never know what drove him on,"
he continued, his voice charged with theatrical
excitement. Clearly he was enjoying himself
hugely. "Was it only the chimera of some hidden
treasure, or did the entity encoffined behind this
portal in some subtle way direct his emotions?
Whatever the truth, he forced his bar into this
crack, even as I am doing, and with one wrench—
the thing was free!"

The splintering crack of the door as it sprang
outward under the prying steel made them all
flinch back reflexively. The door banged to a stop
against the wall and stood gaping, utter blackness
beyond it. From some far part of the house came an
answering echo. Then there was silence except for
the labored breathing of Hale. He tossed down the
crowbar with a ringing clang.

"Nothing," he said. "Did you expect differently? You shouldn't have. Don't you see? It's still
free. When Biddingford ordered this room boarded
up he locked the creature, whatever it is, on the
outside."

A draft stirred the flame of the lamp and
made it flutter. Instead of diminishing, it strength-

ened. Eliza saw Amber's long reddish hair ripple across her face as the other woman clawed at it. Allan bent almost double over the lamp to shield it with his body, cupping his hand around the top of the shade. Dust whipped up from the floor and gritted their eyes.

"It must have a sense of nostalgia," Hale said loudly. "It came back to look at its old room."

Even as he spoke the draft died away. Eliza thought she heard a soft gibbering chatter as the air stilled, but it was so faint she said nothing.

Hale blew out an exclamation of breath.

"Well! No doubt about that manifestation."

"We still have no physical proof," Mohan reminded him. "The skeptics—"

"Damn the skeptics," said Hale. He rubbed his hands briskly. "Let's go in and take a look."

Allan followed quickly after him through the door with the lamp. The rest went in more slowly, Lee bringing up the rear with a protective hand on Eliza's shoulder.

The black sides of the room seemed to swallow the lamplight whole. It was like being inside the belly of a whale. They spread out from one another, the lamp liming the edges of their bodies. Tentative hands reached out through the blackness for walls which could be felt but not seen.

"No wonder they decided it couldn't be used for a storeroom," Amber said. "Imagine trying to find anything in here."

Hale took the lamp from Allan and carried it back and forth across the flat-black enameled floor, bending low in search of some trace. The floor was absolutely empty. Straightening, he went to the wall.

"Come here and look," he said in a moment, excitement catching in his voice.

They clustered about him. He traced with his finger a thin line of silver that wound around the room. Reaching the gap of the doorway, he shut the door. The silver continued across it, no wider than the span of a fine artist's brush.

"This is metallic silver, not paint," he said. "Lee, notice that it runs around the room at roughly heart level."

"A circle of containment," said Lee.

"It must be. Biddingford broke it when he opened the door. The pentacle on the door wasn't designed to keep the entity in. It was a warning to stay out. This was holding it. Only this."

Allan started to chuckle, and then to laugh. Once started he could not stop. The tension in the air made the laughter infectious. Mary giggled. Even Hale smiled weakly.

"What's so funny?" he said.

With an effort of will Allan sobered himself.

"I was thinking," he said. "We were afraid to come in here, but this is probably the only safe room in the house."

"You're right," said Hale. "Now that it's shown itself to us it may feel compelled to attack. But this is one room I think we can safely assume it will never enter."

"Do you think the barrier would still hold it, if we could lure it back into this room?" said Mohan.

"Perhaps," Hale said. "But we don't want to imprison it. That was Brannon's mistake. This thing is evil. It must be destroyed."

That's been his purpose from the beginning, Eliza realized. It's never been his intention merely to study the entity, but to exterminate it. To him we're only tools to achieve that end.

"This is the place I saw," Mary said suddenly. "When I held the pendant."

"Lamen," Hale corrected. "Are you sure?"

"There were marks in the floor that aren't here now, but the atmosphere is the same. I'm sure this is the room."

"This must be the ritual chamber where Brannon and his friends practiced their magic. It makes sense. I wonder how they got in here without alerting the servants?"

"They were likely accomplices," Allan said.

"Yes. Let's go down." Hale turned his watch to the lamp. "It's nearly four o'clock. We can have either a late lunch or an early dinner."

"Thank God—I'm starved," said Amber.

"After we eat we'll get down to the really serious work. We have to find out what's behind all this, and quickly. Our time is running out. With every day that passes this thing gets stronger. Since there are apparently no physical records, we'll have to pursue our inquiries from a different angle."

"A seance?" Mary asked, a drop of fear in her voice.

"Yes Mary, and I'm afraid you'll have to carry the main burden of the work, as well as the danger."

They left the door to the black room open and went down to the kitchen, where Mary set about happily preparing a meal. The cooking chores seemed to drive the apprehension from her mind. Eliza and Mohan offered to help but she fussily waved them off.

"There can't be two cooks in one kitchen," she said. "It's against nature."

Hale got up from the table and wandered restlessly into the passage. Eliza sensed his growing unease but said nothing. After a while she heard a low whistle from somewhere in the front of the house. Amber was joking with Allan. Both stopped to listen. Eliza caught Lee's gaze across the table.

"Where's Luther?" she said.

Hale came back with a troubled look on his bluff, solid face.

"The dog doesn't seem to be in the house. I wonder if you'd mind helping me look for him before we eat. He's probably got himself locked in one of the rooms."

Eliza remembered the fate of the horses and shivered. Hale cared more for the mastiff than he would admit.

They searched the house from top to bottom with no sign of the dog. Then abruptly Mohan gave a shout that brought them all running. He was in a small room in the west wing on the ground floor, just beyond the ballroom. When they arrived he showed them what he had discovered. Two panes of glass were shattered outward from one of the windows, as though a heavy body had hurtled through. Eliza recalled the echo she had heard when the door to the black room banged open. Or had it been an echo?

Hale leaned out the opening and studied the snow beneath the window. He drew in silently. Eliza looked. In the fading twilight she saw drops of scarlet on the white snow, and a line of prints leading around the edge of the house toward the rear lawn.

They're Luther's tracks," Hale said to her mute question. "He must have seen something through the window and chased it."

"We will go after him," Mohan said gently.

"No." Hale turned his back on the window. "It's nearly dark. Luther will have to take his chances. Lee, do you think you could patch this window?"

"I'll close the storm shutters," Lee said.

"Fine. Let's eat, the rest of us. We'll need our strength for tonight."

**9**

Eliza picked at her expandable watch strap and pulled it out, letting it snap back against her wrist. She realized that she was making a red spot on her skin and folded her hands together on the conference table, determined not to fidget. It was after eight o'clock. The tension in the gathering room had increased unbearably. She tried to cut herself off from the emotional turmoil of the others but could not.

They sat silent and apart. Hale and Allan had gone out to prepare the seance. Mohan was at the desk reading, or pretending to read, some of the background material on Haven. Amber lounged with her boots off and her feet up on the couch, shaping her long nails with an emery board. Mary sat in a chair with her hands pressed between her knees staring at the fire. From time to time her lips moved in silent prayer.

Only Lee gave any sign of maintaining an internal balance, and even in his tightly controlled mind Eliza felt a growing anticipation, as though he were preparing himself for an ordeal.

"Would you please stop that scratching?" Eliza said in irritation. "It's driving me crazy."

Amber looked at her a moment, then shrugged and slid the emery board back into her stylish snakeskin purse. She took out a sealed pack of cigarettes and toyed with it meditatively without opening it.

Luther had not returned. Hale had followed the track of the mastiff as far as the edge of the woods. The track led behind the stable in the general direction of the stone quarry. They had eaten with little conversation, taking turns calling the dog from the back door. Somehow the unexplained behavior of the mastiff transformed what had before been partly a game into something more serious.

Hale entered the gathering room and rummaged in one of the cardboard boxes for a fresh video cassette, which he inserted into the camera. He exchanged its partially-depleted battery pack for one that was fully charged.

"We're ready," he said, excitement in his voice. "Follow me, everyone."

They emerged into the front hall. Beneath the crystal chandelier five wooden chairs formed a ring facing inward with a sixth at their center. A double circle of white chalk on the flagstone floor surrounded the chairs at a distance of several feet. The chalk lines ran about six inches apart, and between them words were written in a script Eliza did not recognize. Around the circles a large chalk square had been drawn. Four kerosene lamps sat burning at its corners. Undecipherable words were written in the angles of the square.

A fire burned in the great stone fireplace in the south wall beneath the second-level balcony. Its dancing flames took the chill off the air. The firelight reflecting from the tiles on the hearth gave the mounted stag head an unnatural animation and sent the shadows of its antlers sliding like long black fingers across the walls and ceiling.

"Enter the circle through the gap in the west and take your seats," Hale said. "Leave the seat at the south vacant. Amber and Eliza, sit on either side of the empty chair, please."

Without prompting Mary took the chair in the center, which faced the fireplace. Eliza sat on her right side and Amber on her left. Lee and Mohan sat in the chairs behind Mary. Hale fixed the video camera to a tripod next to the hearth where it would record the seance and turned it on. He entered the circle and sat in the chair to the south facing Mary. Their knees nearly touched.

"Join hands," he said. "And if you value your sanity, don't let go until I tell you."

Eliza took Lee's responsive fingers in her left hand and the rougher fingers of Hale in her right. She sent a glance of encouragement to Mary, who answered with a weak smile.

Allan emerged from the dark entrance of the back passage and crossed in front of the fire. He wore a black pullover sweater and black jeans. In his left hand he carried a small crystal bottle and in his right a smoking brass censor on a triple chain. Pungent incense filled the air.

"Allan will control the seance and erect barriers of protection," Hale murmured.

Allan moved with slow grace, his face strangely distant. He seemed to be in some form of trance. He entered the double circle through the gap, then set the censor and the crystal bottle on the flagstones in the south and used a piece of chalk to join the lines after him. Returning to the south, he extended his right index finger outward and walked once around the chairs clockwise.

"Once seals," he said in a startlingly sonorous voice.

Picking up the smoking censor he repeated the circuit.

"Twice sears."

He exchanged the censor for the crystal bottle, opened it and sprinkled its contents outward as he made yet a third circumambulation.

"Thrice purges."

He approached close behind the chair of Hale and spread his arms. The fire at his back cast his shadow across their upturned faces. His own countenance remained obscure.

"Bornless One, Lord of Earth and Heaven, First and Last, Beginning and End, Alpha and Omega, Thou who art God of gods and Ruler of men, before Whom the stars tremble, within Whom the seas ebb and flow—hear us! Extend Thy infinite mercy upon the task we are about to perform. Into Thy boundless grace we entrust our souls."

He dropped his arms and bowed his head, then began to speak in a lower tone guttural sounds Eliza took to be words but could not recognize. Several of the words he repeated more than once. She felt a chill and shivered. Lee's hand tightened on hers. She reassured him with a slight return of pressure.

Allan raised his head and pointed his index finger directly at Mary, who stared at it stricken with wide eyes, like a bird before a snake.

"Dweller in Darkness, by these words of power I give you leave to speak with the tongue of this woman and tell us why you are bound to this place of earth."

He began to utter a series of harsh names while walking slowly around the chairs inside the circle, his left hand raised straight overhead, his right directed unwaveringly at Mary. Eliza lost count of the number of times he walked behind her. She began to feel dizzy, and a sickness rose from the pit of her stomach. She seemed suspended in darkness, her only contact with reality the pressure on her hands. She became conscious of a rushing overhead, like the sound of great wings.

Mary trembled violently. Her eyes rolled back in her head so that only the whites showed and her stuttering mouth flecked with spittle. She emitted animal noises. It seemed impossible such sounds could issue from a human throat. Eliza felt the pain and terror of the other woman fountain up from a deep fissure in the darkness of her mind. With sudden clarity she realized that when the flow of terror reached the surface Mary would go mad.

"You'll kill her!" she cried. She fought to free herself from the grasping hands on either side.

Allan fixed his dark eyes momentarily upon her. Eliza felt her body go limp. An invisible hand pressed over her lips. She could not speak or resist. She was forced to watch and experience the events unfolding before her.

Standing behind Hale, Allan raised his hands to heaven.

"Speak!"

Mary stopped trembling. Her fleshy body sank in upon itself and she shrank visibly in her chair. Abruptly the terror inside her was gone. A murmur passed between her lips.

"Name yourself," Allan commanded.

"Jen-ny." It was the voice of a little girl.

"Jenny, are you the master of this house?"

Silence. Allan repeated the question.

"No," the voice said.

"Is the master here now?"

Hesitantly—"Yes."

"What is the master's name?"

Mary sat motionless, eyes staring sightlessly into the shadows. Allan repeated the question but got no response.

"Jenny, do you know the name?"

"Yes."

"Why won't you tell us?"

There was a long pause.

"Afraid—of him."

"I can protect you," Allan said. "There's no need to fear. Tell us his name."

Mary shuddered. A new expression molded her features. Her head hung forward and her tongue lolled in the corner of her open mouth. It was the face of an idiot.

"Jenny, can you hear me?"

Mary sat as though deaf.

"Who are you?" Allan said. "Speak—I order you!"

"Bo-Bo," said a slurred male voice.

"How old are you, Bo-Bo?"

"'leven—and a half."

"How did you die?"

"Not dead—"

"You are dead. Remember your death."

Mary's face twisted with mingled pain and confusion.

"Knife—he said it wouldn't hurt."

"Who? The master?"

The confusion intensified.

"Yes."

"Was it Brannon, Bo-Bo?" Allan pressed. "Is Brannon the master?"

"Yes, Bran-non. He hurts us—"

Mary jerked taunt in her chair, her back arching. She screamed and thrashed her head from side to side.

"Mary!"

Allan spread the fingers of his right hand in the air over her head. The ring on his index finger sent forth flashing spears of ruby light that seemed to Eliza's dazzled senses to strike and penetrate into the forehead of the entranced channeler.

Mary straightened in her chair and put her hands on her knees. A cunning expression narrowed her eyes and quirked the corners of her mouth. She looked slowly around, studying them.

"Spirit, what is your name?"

"Won't tell," it said in a high male voice.

"Speak! I command you!"

It looked at Allan with contempt.

"You can't make me."

"Do you mean us harm?"

A smile crept across Mary's lips.

"Maybe."

"Are you Daniel P. Brannon?"

It laughed.

A chill went through Eliza. It was the same laughter she had heard on the lawn yesterday.

"How many of you are there?"

It toyed with its fingers for a few minutes as though considering whether to answer.

"Two," it said at last.

"You're lying. Speak the truth."

Slowly it raised its head and looked at Allan with glittering malignancy. Its face was utterly altered.

"You don't know anything, murderer," it said in a deep guttural voice. "We're going to play a game, and when we finish you'll be dead."

Allan pointed at the spot between Mary's eyebrows.

"Speak the truth or I'll burn you with fire."

"We are one, and we are two, and we're too much for the likes of you," it sang, once more using its child's voice.

"How old are you?"

"Thirteen."

"How did you die?"

"Better than you."

"Why are there so many children here?"

"They're locked in and can't get out."

"You got out."

"I'm cleverer than the rest."

"And stronger?"

Again the voice deepened.

"Much stronger."

"Was it you who started the fire in the ball-room?"

It leaned back and looked at the ceiling, sly pleasure stealing across its face.

"You should have heard them scream and run about. Squawk! Squawk!" It flapped its arms. "Like chickens with their tails alight."

"Why don't you go away? You don't belong here."

It stared at Allan with brooding anger.

"Can't," it said in its child voice, and its deeper voice repeated, "Can't. We're bound."

"You escaped the black room. Brannon can't hold you any longer."

"Not by Brannon."

"What binds you to this place, if not Brannon?"

It looked steadily at him.

"Each other," it said.

Abruptly the door to the east wing slammed shut with a thunderous boom.

"No escape for you," it said in its two voices together.

Allan ignored the sound of the door.

"Why did Brannon imprison you?"

"He needed us."

"For what?"

"Mur-der," it said, caressing the word with its lips.

"Who did you kill?"

"Many men."

"Why?"

It was silent.

"What power did Brannon hold over you?"

Again it refused to reply. It twisted in its chair as though seeking escape, turning its leering face to each of them around the circle.

"Who are you?" Allan demanded.

"The fires of hell!"

A great roaring issued from the mouth of the fireplace, and a yellow ribbon of flame slid serpent-like through the air and twined itself around them. As it continued to wind over and over its own length, it thickened. The air outside the boundary of the circle was filled with heat and light.

"Hold your places!" Hale cried.

The whirling flame formed a solid wall and pressed in upon them. Eliza squeezed her eyes shut against the blinding brightness and gulped the searing air. The skin on her back crackled. A smell of burning flesh filled her nostrils. She blinked back tears of pain and looked at Hale for guidance.

Hale was staring at Mary as though mesmerized. Some strange transformation had come upon her. Fire wreathed her head and her eyes blazed like twin stars. Through the shimmering waves of heat her face enlarged and distorted, becoming bestial.

The house is burning, Eliza thought calmly. We're all going to die. They'll find our bodies in the ashes. Will mamma weep when the doctors at the institution tell her? If she's having one of her bad days, will she even understand?

Numbness settled over her emotions and soothed them. She no longer felt pain. The roaring of the flames receded and her awareness drifted apart from her body. She looked down and saw herself and the others straining forward in their chairs, their hands still joined, faces wide with fear. She could see everyone at once from every angle, as though she were a million places at the same instant. Strangely, she could not see the fire.

She watched Allan turn and face the edge of the circle as though confronting some invisible menace. Shouting barbarous words, he tore the heavy silver ring from his finger and cast it out through the barrier. A flash of pure white light stunned her senses.

Eliza opened her eyes. Hands were raising her upright in her chair. She saw Mary lying as though dead on the floor at her feet and reached down to help her.

"Let me," Hale said. "You're too weak."

He crouched and cradled the head of the unconscious woman in his hands while Mohan knelt over her chaffing her hand anxiously.

"Poor little Mary," Mohan muttered in distress.

She groaned and struggled feebly, then relaxed and opened her eyes.

"It was bad," she whispered. "I knew it would be."

Eliza looked around in wonder. There was no trace of the curtain of flame. Everything was as before. The fire still burned on the hearth. The lamps still flickered in the corners of the chalk square. Only the members of the group had changed. They were drenched in sweat and trembling with fatigue. She realized with a start of surprise that she was in exactly the same condition.

Allan supported himself on the back of Hale's chair. His blanched face bore a haggard look.

"No one leave the circle," he said. "Not until I exorcise the room."

He walked once around the circle counterclockwise with his finger pointing outward, muttering words in an unknown tongue. Returning to the south, he flung wide his arms in a gesture of banishment.

"All spirits drawn to this circle, depart! In the name of the Bornless One I exorcise and compel thee!"

He clapped his hands four times sharply together, then paused with his head cocked as though listening. He relaxed slowly.

"It's safe to step out."

When Mary began to recover, Allan helped Hale lift her into a chair and Mohan ran to get a damp cloth from the kitchen. He returned and tenderly wiped her face and neck.

"You will be all right," he told her gently. "No, do not try to stand up yet."

"I hope you learned something, Professor," Mary said with a wan smile.

"A great deal." Hale looked around at the others. "I want everyone to record their impressions. Everything you saw, heard, felt, smelled, tasted or imagined. We'll correlate tomorrow."

Allan walked over and picked up his ring from where it had fallen. He turned it over and examined it.

"If I hadn't interrupted the circuit of the flow with this, I don't know what would have happened," he told Hale.

"How did you know what to do?" Lee asked.

Allan shrugged.

"Something touched me. I can't explain it. I felt an inner direction."

"Write it down," Hale said wearily. "We wanted phenomena. Tonight we got phenomena."

"I'm not so sure," said Lee.

"How do you mean?"

"Look around." He gestured across the hall. "No damage. Nothing is even disturbed."

"I thought my hair was on fire," Amber said to Eliza. She stroked it and lifted it from her shoulder. "Look, it's not even singed."

"I see what you mean," Hale said to Lee. "It was merely an illusion to test our nerve. As the entity said, it was playing with us."

"But the game is deadly. If one of us had run outside the circle—"

Hale went over to shut off the video camera.

"If the fire existed we'll see it when we play this tape."

A distant wailing howl froze him motionless. They listened until it ended, staring from one to another.

"What is it?" Amber whispered. "A wolf?"

Hale switched off the camera and methodically unhooked it from the tripod.

"It's Luther," he said.

# 10

"I've gone over your accounts of last night," Hale said, dropping a pile of papers on the table. "It seems a divergence exists between what we experienced and what actually took place."

They sat around the conference table in the gathering room. It was early afternoon of Christmas day. Shadowless gray light flooded through the tall windows from an overcast sky.

"I want you to look at the tape I made of the seance."

He pressed the playback switch on the camera and they watched the small television screen while their own recorded voices, first tense and later shrill, filled the room. When it was over he turned the machine off.

"Any comments?"

Eliza took a deep breath and tried to still the tremble in her hands by pressing them flat on the table. The tape had revived the emotions of the other night. They buffeted against her mind like storm winds.

109

"There was no trace of the fire," she said, speaking for the rest.

"Exactly," Hale said. "Lee's intuition was correct. The fire was a psychic event."

"But we heard the voices of the spirits," said Amber.

"Because they came from Mary's vocal apparatus. But notice that the changes in her features several of you reported seeing toward the end of the experiment were not recorded by the camera."

He got up and went to the chalkboard, dragging it farther away from the tree so that he could walk around it. He drew a thick chalk line down its center.

"Let's run through the things we know about the supernatural events at Haven." He waved the chalk. "Anyone?"

"There's more than one entity," Amber said.

"Four that we know." Hale began to write on the left side of the board. "Jenny. Bo-Bo. And two others who appear to be linked in some way."

"Three of the voices were childlike," Lee said.

"How would you characterize the fourth?"

"Bestial. Inhuman."

"The double entity appears to be the source of the events," said Allan.

"The primary source, at least," Hale agreed. "Anything else?"

"It is capable of some physical phenomena," said Mohan in his soft flowing accent. "There were the footprints seen by Eliza. And the statement by George Three-Rivers that something tried to drown Mrs. Biddingford in her bath."

"And its physical strength may increase toward the end of the year," added Hale, jotting the points down.

"It has an affinity for fire," said Eliza. "Its hair and eyes were burning. It threatened us with flame, and it caused the fire in the west wing."

Hale wrote "Salamander" and put a question mark after it.

"A Salamander is the name for a fire elemental," Lee murmured to Eliza, who was seated beside him.

"It's evil," Mary said in a low voice. "It intends to kill us."

"It has power over animals," Allan said.

Hale noted this without speaking. He had spent part of the morning walking through the woods calling Luther. The erratic, winding track of the mastiff through the snow suggested that it had run mad.

"We can surmise that this entity was called into being by Daniel P. Brannon for purposes unknown, imprisoned in the black room for nearly half a century, then released inadvertently by Biddingford," Lee offered.

"And that Brannon was part of some cult or secret society," said Amber.

"That Brannon was a skilled theurgist," said Allan.

"Anything more?"

They were silent.

"All right," said Hale after a few moments. "Let's list those things we don't know. What are our major questions?"

"What is it?" said Allan.

Hale wrote "name(s)—nature" on the right side of the chalkboard.

"What does it want?" said Mary.

Hale wrote "purpose."

"Why was it called into manifestation?" Lee said. "And why does it get more aggressive and violent toward the end of the year?"

Hale continued jotting.

"For what reason does it remain at Haven?" said Mohan.

"When will it be strong enough to kill us?" Allan said quietly.

Hale looked at him a moment, then wrote "strength."

"Is that it?"

"When do we open our presents?" said Amber.

Laughter diffused the tension. Eliza looked at the small pile of packages that lay under the boughs of the crudely decorated tree. Some had been there when she came down for breakfast, and the pile had quickly grown in the early hours of the morning. She had selected six of her personal possessions and wrapped them in plain notepaper, adding them to the rest. It was the first time anyone had mentioned the presents.

"Let's wait until after dinner," said Hale with a smile. "I understand Mary has something special planned."

Mary blushed and dropped her eyes. Eliza felt the inner glow of pleasure in the other woman.

She suspected that Mary had been the first to plant gifts under the tree.

"I also have a little secret I've been saving for tonight," Allan said mysteriously.

"What is it?" asked Amber.

"You'll find out with the rest, my lovely little witch."

A distant scraping and banging stopped further conversation. They listened silently for several moments.

"It's coming from the back door," said Lee.

The banging was followed by a series of deep barks.

"It's Luther," Hale said.

He ran out of the room, knocking over the chalkboard easel in his haste.

"Professor, be careful!" Lee called after him.

Eliza followed Lee across the flagstones of the front hall with the others close on her heels. She rounded the entrance to the rear passageway just in time to see Hale unbolt and open the outer door.

"Wait—" Lee shouted.

The door burst inward with tremendous force and knocked Hale onto his back. The great body of the mastiff landed on top of him. Eliza parted her lips to scream.

"Good dog, good dog," Hale said, laughing.

The long tongue of the animal laved his face and hands and its tail beat against his shins. He pushed it off his chest and stood up to brush the snow from his sweater, then led the panting dog by its broad leather collar into the kitchen.

Eliza could not help laughing at Lee's reaction. He glanced at her ruefully as the others pressed past them.

"Oh!" Marry exclaimed. "Look at his poor paws."

The dog limped as it danced around Hale. Spots of blood dotted the white ceramic tiles. Eliza saw that its brick-colored fur was caked in places with dry blood.

"You've been in a scrap, haven't you, boy," Hale said, kneeling to examine the dog's coat.

"I'll get the first-aid kit," Mary said.

Eliza picked up one of the dog dishes and filled it with fresh water at the sink. She set it down and Luther lapped at it greedily.

"I thought he was dead," Hale said, patting the dog on the side.

"What do you think happened?" said Lee. "Temporary possession?"

Hale nodded.

"It seems likely. If he'd been chasing something he would have come back last night. His tracks lead all over the woods. The poor mutt was almost run to death."

"It looks as though he was digging," said Eliza. "Only his front paws are cut."

"Little wonder with this frozen ground," Hale said.

He went to a window and peered out.

"There's a trail of blood in the snow. I'm going to follow it. Anyone like to go with me?"

They all volunteered.

Hale pulled on rubber overshoes and took from the rack behind the kitchen door a quilted nylon jacket of drab olive-green.

"Mary, I want you to look after Luther. You have to prepare dinner in any case. And Mohan, I'd like you to stay with her so she won't be left alone."

Mary nodded and continued to sponge the blood from between the toes of the dog with a cotton swab.

"I will make sure she is safe," Mohan promised.

In a short while Eliza found herself following Hale through the woods, the house lost from sight behind the trees. It was not as cold as yesterday. The snow squeezed rather than crunched under her boots. The shadowless light of the overcast sky made the distant forested mountains look like an impressionistic charcoal sketch.

Allan and Amber kept up a running snow fight, and periodically the others were drawn in. Their shouts and laughter rang out harshly on the stillness. It was only when they had walked for some time that Eliza recognized with a start the direction the bloody prints were leading.

"They go to the stone quarry," she said.

"If the dog was digging there it's a wonder it can still walk," said Allan. "It's nothing but broken granite."

They continued on in silence to the stand of stunted spruce at the edge of the quarry where Eliza had nearly fallen.

"Be carefully," she warned. "It's treacherous."

She looked around uneasily. It was just about here that the thing must have stood watching her. The small hairs on the back of her neck prickled. She hunched her shoulders inside her coat.

They pressed through the springy spruce branches and stepped into the uneven bowl of the quarry.

"Here," said Hale, walking over and crouching.

The snow and rocks were covered with a spatter of red for several feet around. It looked as though a small animal had been butchered on the spot.

"This is where Luther was digging. Give me a hand."

Hale began throwing aside the jagged stones. Some were as small as he fist. Others required the full effort of the three men to drag and roll aside.

Amber and Eliza dusted off the tops of two boulders some distance away and sat watching with the rough face of the cliff at their backs. After a while Amber folded back the hood of her fur coat and shook out her auburn hair across her shoulders. She rummaged in her snakeskin purse and glanced inquiringly at Eliza.

"Cigarette?"

"I don't smoke."

"Very wise. It's a filthy habit. I'm trying to quit myself."

She shut the silver clasp of the purse with a decisive snap.

"Want some chocolate?"

There was a note of uncertainty in her husky voice. Eliza realized the candy was meant as a peace offering.

"Sure."

She accepted half of a broken chocolate bar, still in its wrapper. It was dark with almonds and raisins. They ate quietly for a time.

"This place gives me the willies," Amber said at last.

"I know what you mean," Eliza agreed between nibbles.

"I've got half a mind to pack a suitcase and start walking down the coast."

"You wouldn't make it. A person needs special gear to survive in the woods in winter."

"What makes you an authority?"

"I used to live in Saskatoon."

"It is cold there?"

"Oh yes."

Amber balled up her piece of candy wrapper and threw it over her shoulder against the rock. She gave a short laugh.

"What's so funny?"

"I usually spend Christmas in Acapulco."

"You're a warm water rat."

"What's that?"

"My father used to say there were warm water rats and cold water rats."

"And I suppose you're the cold water variety."

"I guess so."

"Which kind is Lee?"

Eliza watched Lee hurl a stone onto a growing pile.

"I haven't decided."

"I think he's tepid," Amber said. "I never met such a bloodless male in my life."

"You get along all right with Allan."

Amber studied her mildly.

"We're comfortable with each other. Allan and I come from the same background."

"What's that?"

"Country clubs. Private riding schools. Vacations in Europe."

Eliza looked at Allan curiously. He was wrestling with a stone too heavy for him. His slender back twisted with effort inside his loose navy pea jacket, which seemed several sizes too big. Lee helped him lift the rock from the hole.

"I didn't think he was the country club type."

"I know," Amber said. "But his father is absolutely stinking rich. The old man disinherited him when he found out about Allan's occult activities."

"Just because he studies magic?"

"Not only that." Amber dropped her voice. "I shouldn't be telling you this, but a couple of years ago Allan was involved with the authorities in Spain. Some underage girl died during an occult ritual he was conducting. The police tried to implicate him."

"What happened?"

"I'm not sure. Allan wouldn't say. But I think it still troubles him."

Eliza remembered that during the seance the entity had called Allan a murderer. It had puzzled her at the time. Now she understood. It attacks us at our weak points, she thought.

"At least he's got a father," Amber said with a trace of bitterness. "My parents divorced when I was five. I barely remember my father. My mother remarried when I was nine. He married her for money. Every time my mother got drunk he came after me. For three years it was pure hell. Then I was sent away to a boarding school in Europe. I avoid home as much as I can. During the summers I travel and do a little fashion modeling."

"How did you become a witch?" Eliza asked to change the subject.

"Through my grandmother," Amber said, smiling at the memory. "She was a Theosophist and a spirit medium. She claimed to have known Madam Blavatsky personally. Once she even met Aleister Crowley, but she wasn't very impressed. She used to tell me all about Sarah Wildes, an ancestral black sheep of the family hanged for witchcraft at Salem. After my mother remarried, my step-father wouldn't let me visit her. She's dead now."

Eliza closed her eyes and tilted her face toward the sky. The gray light filtered gently through her lids.

"My father died when I was eighteen. He owned a small retail business in western Canada. My mother never got over his death. Gradually she lost control of her mind, became schizophrenic. She's in an institution in Toronto. At times she's almost normal. Other days she doesn't even know who I am."

"I'm sorry," Amber said.

Eliza shrugged and opened her eyes.

"I wonder what Mary and Mohan are doing," she said in a lighter voice.

"Probably upstairs in one of the beds."

"Amber!"

"Well I think he's sweet on her," Amber said, eyes bright with mischief. "You saw the way he acted when she fainted after the seance."

"That doesn't prove anything."

"No? I've heard about these Hindus. They have deeply passionate souls."

"I thought he was a Sikh."

"Don't use facts to confuse the issue."

"Sex is all you think about, isn't it?"

"What else is there?"

The digging stopped. Eliza noticed the silence and turned to look. Lee waved her and Amber over.

They approached the men, who stood looking down into the shallow hole they had excavated in the loose rock. When Eliza followed their gaze she saw peeking from between the jumbled stones the smooth dome of a human skull. It was lying on its side. One eye socket and some upper teeth were visible.

"It said it had killed," Allan murmured.

Hale pulled off his green stocking cap and used it to wipe the sweat from his eyebrows before putting it back on. He stepped heavily into the trench and worked the skull loose, holding it up for examination on his gloved palm.

"It's so small," said Amber.

"The skull of a small woman or a child," Hale said.

"I wonder if there are any others?" Lee looked at the stones under Hale's boots, then met the older man's eyes.

"Only one way to find out," said Hale.

They continued to dig, passing up the bones they uncovered to Eliza and Amber, who paced the rim of the deepening pit. by the time the light began to fail the men had dug down to breast level. Nine skulls, all of children, formed a mound along with numerous other ivory-colored bones.

"We'd better quit," Hale said at last. He climbed out with difficulty. "We don't want to be caught in the woods after dark."

"Shouldn't we take the bones back with us?" asked Amber.

Hale looked at them and shook his head.

"No. Best to leave them for the Mounties. I'll contact them when we get back to Regret Cove."

He went into the woods and kicked a small fallen tree loose from the frost. With the help of Allan and Lee he propped it upright next to the bones in a pile of rocks.

"This will mark them," he said, dusting the bark from his gloves. He squinted at the sky. "It feels like more snow."

Even as he spoke Eliza saw a tiny crystal land on the green wool of his cap. It remained there without melting.

"This is a damnable business," Hale said sadly. "Worse than I ever imagined."

They were subdued as they followed their trail through the woods back to Haven. By the time the house reared into sight above the trees it was snowing heavily through the twilight gloom.

A pleasant smell of cooking odors greeted them as they entered the kitchen. Mohan and Mary were both present. Luther lay by the stove. While they hung up their coats, Hale described briefly what had been found in the quarry.

Mary was shocked and frightened. Mohan seemed strangely unmoved.

"I am not surprised," he said in a solemn voice. "It fits all too well the information I have uncovered."

"What have you found out?" Hale asked.

"Well, you know I have been studying the records of Haven and its owners searching for clues that might be of use to us."

"Yes, go on."

Mohan took a typed legal-size sheet of paper from the Kitchen table.

"Daniel P. Brannon founded a children's hospital in the year 1896."

"He was a philanthropist," Allan said. "He founded many charities."

"Yes, but this one is different. I have checked. All the others had to do with social or cultural institutions. Libraries. Monuments. Art galleries. Gymnasiums."

He handed Hale the paper and pointed midway down the list.

"This is the only one that has to do with sickness or infirmity, and the only one to concern children."

"What was the name of the hospital?" asked Lee.

"The Brannon Asylum For the Juvenile Insane."

Hale frowned and passed the paper around.

"I'm not sure I see your point," he said. "Where is the connection with Haven?"

"That is the point exactly," said Mohan. His eyes lit with excitement. "It was the miniature furniture that first made me wonder. I checked most carefully. All the other charities established by Brannon have addresses, but there is no address listed for the Asylum."

Eliza felt a knot form in the pit of her stomach.

"I still don't understand," said Hale.

"What reason could Brannon have for not wishing the address of the Asylum widely circulated?" said Mohan.

Hale stared at him, comprehension at last beginning to dawn.

"It is because the address of the Asylum and Brannon's home address were one and the same."

"You mean," Lee said, "Haven was once—"

"A madhouse for children."

11

Christmas dinner was made up of a thick lightly-seasoned cream soup, baked canned ham with an apricot glazing, baked potatoes, mixed vegetables, freshly made tea biscuits smothered in butter, strong tea, and for desert a rich fruit pudding with a sauce of sweetened cream.

They looked at the pudding as though it were an apparition from another world when Mary bore it steaming from the oven and began dividing it into the Victorian china desert bowls.

"How on earth did you manage to make a pudding out of our supplies?" Hale asked. "Everything is canned, dried or powdered."

"We had flour and sugar. Powdered eggs. Canned milk. Salt. Dried fruit. There's not much else a smart cook needs," Mary said with a trace of pride as she ladled out the sauce.

"This is wonderful," said Eliza. "It wouldn't have seemed like Christmas without a real cooked meal."

"I agree," Allan said expansively. "Mary, you've taken some of the horror from this depressing old pile."

There was a general concurrence with his opinion. Mary blushed but seemed pleased over the attention in her quiet way.

They left the dishes and pots for Hale to wash the following morning and went with their lamps into the gathering room, where a low fire glowed on the grate. Luther got up from the hearth and came over to lick the hand of his master. Hale examined the mastiff as he patted its thick neck.

"He seems stronger," he said to Eliza. "I think he'll be all right."

"Let's open the presents," Amber said.

"First my surprise," said Allan. He went to a cardboard box by the desk and pulled from it three dusty bottles, cradling them carefully in his hands.

"Wine!" said Amber, wide-eyed. "Where on earth did you get it?"

Allan passed her a bottle and twisted the cork from one of his own. The seals were already broken. He began to pour the sparkling golden liquid into long-stemmed crystal goblets set out on an end table.

"I was exploring," he said, holding the bottle to the firelight to gauge the progress of the sediment. "I happened to go into the cellar. All kinds of junk down there. I found a box of white wine. It had been left standing upright and the corks were dry. All but these three bottles had gone to vinegar." He smiled. "Naturally I had to test them. That's why the seals are broken."

"It's perfectly good," Amber said, draining a glass she had half-filled from her bottle.

The spirits of the group were lifted another notch by the wine. Eliza felt the flood of emotions from the others buoy her up. They opened their gifts and exchanged complements with more sincerity than seemed possible only a few hours before. The wine possessed a mysterious energizing power. The shadows retreated before its clear sparkle. Even Mary drank several glasses and began to talk and laugh freely.

"What I don't understand," said Allan, "Is why Brannon would turn his own house into an institution."

"We may never know, unless there's some clue at Haven we haven't uncovered yet," Lee said. He stretched his sock feet across the low table in front of the couch toward the fire.

"It's possible," Hale said. "Without roads it costs a fortune to move anything in or out of Haven, as I mentioned before. When something comes it usually stays."

"We should search the house from top to bottom," suggested Mohan.

Hale shook his head lazily on the padded back of his chair and closed his eyes.

"Impractical. It would take weeks to do a thorough job. Maybe months."

"I don't think this thing, whatever it is—" Amber began.

"Let's call it our adversary," Hale suggested.

"I don't think this adversary has any real power. Not in a physical sense. If it had it would have done something before now."

"I agree," Lee said. "All the phenomena we've experienced or have read accounts of have been physically minor."

"The fire in the ballroom," Mary objected.

"A single spark might have started it. The panicking guests probably knocked over the tree trying to get out of the way."

Eliza curled her toes at the fire. She had taken off her boots and sat on the couch beside Lee.

"Even so," she said, "One spark during the night while we sleep would be enough to finish us."

"That would destroy Haven," Hale said. "I doubt it wants to do that. Haven is its home, its refuge, perhaps its prison."

"If only I knew its name," Allan said. "I might be able to work against it. Bind it. Exorcise it."

"It's crafty," Lee agreed. "But there may be a way to find out."

"You have a plan of attack?" said Allan.

"Maybe."

Hale let his hand fall to the leather armrest of his chair with a loud bang. Luther started and looked at him.

"Let it wait 'til morning. It's late. We're all tired, and I suspect a trifle drunk—at least I know I am. Let's go to bed."

They gathered their things and carried their lamps upstairs, bidding each other good night in the corridor.

Eliza entered her room and closed the door over without clicking it into place. She dropped her armful of gifts on the bureau as she passed it, then sat heavily on the bed and with exaggerated care placed her lamp on the floor where she would not kick it over. Her head spun in a pleasant way. She heard the snow hissing against the window behind her. Even though Allan had left the gathering room an hour ago to do the rounds lighting the kerosene heaters, her room still held a deep chill that made her shiver.

She changed into her strawberry pajamas and took a trip to the bathroom. The corridor was empty, all the doors closed. Returning to her room, she was about to blow out the lamp when a creak from the floorboards outside her door froze her motionless in a sitting position on the bed. She watched with mounting tension the door silently open inward.

It was Lee. He wore dark pajama bottoms and a white terry cloth robe with black trim that hung open to reveal the curling hairs on his naked chest. His feet were bare. He smiled apologetically at her expression.

"Sorry I scared you," he whispered, closing the door after him.

"What do you want?" she said in a low voice. She was acutely conscious that Amber was only a wall away.

"The same thing as you, I hope. If I'm wrong tell me and I'll leave."

She said nothing. The buzz of the wine in her head made it hard to think. She became aware of his warmth as he sat on the bed beside her.

"I wanted to come last night," he said softly, taking her hand. "But I wasn't sure."

"Are you sure now?"

She did not draw her hand away.

"I'm sure I want you."

He put his arm over her shoulder and drew her closer. She stood up and faced him.

"This is a bit of a surprise," she said, flustered. "You were so reserved. Amber even thought—" She stopped.

He smiled slowly.

"Did she tell you about that?"

Eliza nodded.

"I thought maybe you were celibate—you know, under a vow of some kind."

He put his hand over his mouth and fell slowly back across the mattress, his stomach and sides shaking. Eliza realized that he was laughing. Indignation bit her.

"I'm sorry," he whispered, sitting up and wiping the tears from his eyes. "That's so funny."

"Well what were we supposed to think when you sent her away?" she said angrily.

"Amber's a beautiful woman, but she's not for me," he said, looking at her with sudden sincerity. He reached out and took her two hands.

"Am I?" She began to breath more quickly.

He stood and kissed her on the lips. His hands slid up her back to embrace her. Trembling, she broke away.

"What's wrong, Eliza?" he said, puzzled.

She breathed deeply without meeting his eyes, feeling her color come and go. Her fingers covered her lips.

"I can't," she whispered.

"Why not?" Gently he pulled her hand down and made her look at him. "Is it me?"

"No, no." How could she explain the apprehension inside her? He would never understand.

"Tell me."

She felt tears start in her eyes and fought them away.

"I'm an empath. You don't know what that means. I feel things deeply, too deeply. Not only my own emotions but those of other people."

"I assumed you could control it."

"I can most of the time, but not—" She fought for the words. "Not when it becomes personal. I feel every suspicion, every reproach, every anger. And it hurts, Lee, God how it hurts."

He stroked the soft honey curls of her hair.

"Haven't you ever had a lover?"

"Once. I tried to make it work. It was no good—no good for either of us."

"He let you down?"

She nodded.

"I don't blame him. He found someone else. Someone normal. He didn't have the courage to tell me straight out, so we dragged on together for a while. It became terribly bitter at the end."

"It could be different."

"No." She closed her eyes and shook her head. "I can't bear that pain again."

She felt his hand slid away from her body. Suddenly she was cold. Opening her eyes, she saw that he had moved to the door.

"We'll leave it this way for tonight," he said. "But I haven't given up."

Eliza could not reply. She watched the door close behind him. After several seconds she blew out the lamp and climbed under the chill blankets on the bed. She cried herself to sleep.

Darkness stretched into darkness around her. Voices whispered encouraging words. Laughter cascaded in a distant shower like the song of birds. She walked down the endless incline of a great invisible spiral. Far above her, hidden from her sight, the stars twinkled in the hollow vault of space. She felt utter freedom. No walls of flesh held her in. No eyes blinded her. No ears made her deaf to the music sighing up from below, drawing her deeper into the loving darkness.

"Will we be in time?" said a fearful voice without inflection.

"Hurry," said another. "While it wanders, while it works, we are safe."

"Safe," echoed several voices.

"It will hurt us," said yet another.

"No matter," the first replied. "We must help."

"Help." Like a rustle on an autumn day.

Eliza felt a pressure grow around her and bear her down. It was as though she had passed into a breathless cavern under the roots of a mountain. A vastness of earth oppressed her heart. She could no longer walk but crawled through the midnight void without hands or feet. No question arose within her mind. She was as passive and accepting as a child rocked in its mother's arms. She felt only a quiet sense of wonder.

"She has it. She takes it up," the third voice exulted.

"Quickly, guide her back before it sees," said the second.

"It returns, it watches," said the first in alarm.

"Too late, too late," they sighed in chorus like the wind in the trees.

Eliza felt herself rise weightless through space, returning upward toward the glittering stars. In her arms she clutched something square and hard. As she neared the surface rude fingers tried to tear it away from her grasp, but she held on and fought furiously. Eventually the fingers withdrew and she knew she had won a victory, though what kind or how great she could not imagine. Her mind broke the mirror of darkness like the head of a swimmer rising for breath.

"Eliza, wake up."

She opened her eyes.

Lee was leaning over the bed with a look of concern, his hand on her shoulder.

"What is it?" she murmured. "What's wrong?"

Blinking owlishly, she realized it was morning. The chill gray light from the window showed him already dressed in a denim shirt and jeans.

"It's Mary," he said with a hollow voice.

She sensed his emotions and grabbed his arms. "Is she hurt?"

"She's dead."

Eliza sat up slowly. Her feelings drained away and left her numb.

"I'll get dressed."

"Amber found her," Lee said. "She was in her room on the bed."

Eliza took off her pajamas and mechanically put on a yellow shirt and her rust-colored corduroy slacks, unconscious that she was making herself nearly naked before Lee. She moved in a daze. Mary had been so cheerful the night before. It was impossible to comprehend.

"What's this?" asked Lee.

He picked up a flat black book from the quilted coverlet of the bed and held it toward her. She looked at it.

"I don't know."

Flickers of her dream danced and swirled away from her awareness when she tried to grasp them. Then they were gone.

Lee opened the cover of the book and examined the first page absently. He seemed not to see it. Suddenly his attention quickened. He stared at Eliza.

"Do you know what this is?"

"I don't even know how it got there," she said indifferently, her mind filled with Mary.

"This is Brannon's magical diary," he said in excitement. "At least, I think it is. Come on—we have to show Hale."

She followed him down the corridor to Mary's room. It was tucked under the stairs that led to the attic. The door stood open. Eliza entered and stopped behind the others, who were gathered inside in a semicircle looking down at the bed.

Hale bent beside the bed to pick up something that glittered. As he straightened and stepped aside, Eliza saw Mary. She lay under the covers as though asleep. Blood stained her face and pooled in her upward staring eyes. More blood reddened the pillow and matted her brown hair.

"She was bludgeoned," Hale said. "It looks like it happened sometime near morning."

He examined what he had taken from the floor in the chill window light. Mary's crucifix. Eliza saw that its gold chain was broken. She realized with a sick feeling that it had been torn from the neck of the dead woman. Wordlessly Hale gathered the chain together and set the cross on top of a worn pocket Bible on the table next to the bed.

"This damn house," Allan said between his teeth. "I say we burn it to the ground."

"Wait a minute," Hale said. "This is a police matter now. However it may have happened a woman has been murdered."

"Are you going to radio the village?" Amber asked. Her voice was toneless.

"Yes. I'll do it now. There should be a boat here before noon."

"Good," said Amber. "I'm getting out of this damned place."

"We all are," Hale said wearily. "The seminar is terminated."

He reached down and gently closed the staring eyes of the corpse. Lee detained him as he was going out of the room and showed him the book.

"Brannon's magical diary," he said.

Hale frowned as he forced his attention to focus on the book.

"Where did you find it?"

Lee did not answer.

"It was on my bed when I woke up," Eliza said. "It must have been put there last night while I was asleep."

Hale studied her a moment.

"Keep it safe," he said to Lee. "I can't think now. I'll look at it later."

He continued on to the radio room. His heavy footsteps sounded on the stairs over a corner of the ceiling.

"Better just leave her," Lee said, pulling Mohan gently away from the bed.

Mohan would not or could not look away from the face of the corpse. At last he allowed Lee to guide him to the wall, where he stood gazing into space like a bronze statue.

Eliza went to him. They were some distance from the others, who gathered around the bed.

"Mohan, I know how you felt—" she murmured so that only he could hear. She stopped. What could she say that would comfort him.

"She will be reborn," he whispered. "We all live again."

"It's horrible!" Amber expelled the words with the full force of her revulsion.

"We were fools to misjudge it," Allan said quietly. "It was playing with us. It had the power to kill us all along."

"I'm not sure," said Lee, searching the wound on the head of the dead woman. He reached into her hair and plucked something from the blood, holding it up.

"What is that?" Mohan asked.

"A splinter."

They looked at him blankly.

"Mary wasn't killed by a ghost. Her head was bashed in with a wooden club of some kind."

"What are you saying?" Eliza said.

Lee stuck the bloody splinter on the pillow beside Mary's head.

"I think it was one of us."

They were silent as his words slowly sunk home.

"Possession," said Allan. "Is that what you mean?"

Lee nodded.

"It took one of us during the night, the same way it took Luther, and used that person to kill."

"If that's true," said Amber, "We can't be sure it isn't still inside that person."

"Agreed. We must all be very careful."

Eliza saw an image of herself walking through darkness. When she tried to recapture it, the image vanished into a million fragments. She felt sickness in her throat. The room was heavy with the smell of blood.

"I have to get out."

Blinking spots of faintness from her eyes, she stumbled toward the door.

Hale caught her in his arms and held her. There was a wild look on his face.

"We can't call the police," he said. "The radio's been smashed to pieces."

# 12

"We have to come to a decision," Hale said. "Do we hold out here until the boat comes? Do we send someone to the village? Or do we all pack up and take out chances in the snow?"

They sat tensely around the kitchen table. Eliza stirred the charred logs in the stove and tried to make them burn, but she did not have Mary's touch. The kindling smoldered and fumed.

"Let me," Allan said. He took the poker from her hand.

Eliza went to a window and stared blankly out at the snow. With the accumulation of last night it now carpeted the ground more than a foot deep—twice that in the drifts. There was no sign of life. In her mind an image arose of Mary lying in bed behind the closed door of her room, her lips white, the window open to the frigid winter air. Would the birds fly in when they discovered it open? There were crows in the woods, and smaller birds that looked like starlings.

"I say we leave," said Amber. "I'd take the woods any day over this place."

"That's what it wants," Lee said. "It's trying to make us panic."

"You think we should stay and fight?" asked Allan.

Lee nodded.

"Last night I was going to suggest another seance to learn the name of the entity, but without Mary ..."

"I don't think it makes sense for us all to go," Hale said, his brow knitting in indecision. "The snow's deep. there are no trails. It's going to be two or three tough days travel along the coast."

"If a storm came up or the temperature dropped we wouldn't stand a chance," said Eliza.

They watched each other uneasily. A reserve stood between them that had not existed the day before. Eliza sensed their suspicions, their unasked questions, simmering like a poison.

"There's enough emergency supplies to equip one person adequately and still leave something in reserve." Hale tapped his fingernails meditatively on the table. "I'm willing to send a volunteer."

Lee and Allan exchanged looks.

"I'll go if you like," Lee said. "But I still think we're better off to stand and fight."

"My feelings are the same as Lee's," Allan said.

"Let me go," said Mohan, breaking his long silence. "I believe I can reach the village in one day."

"That's impossible," said Amber. "It's over thirty miles by land."

Mohan regarded her with solemn eyes.

"None the less I can do it. I am a Sikh of the Punjab. My father was a diplomatic aid at the royal court of Nepal. Since the age of three I have studied yoga under Tibetan masters who fled south to escape the Communist occupation of their homeland. They taught me the secrets of tumo and lung-gom."

"Tumo is the ability to generate internal body heat at will," explained Hale. "Lung-gom is the power of crossing great distances in short periods by means of a sort of leaping run."

"Mohan, you'll kill yourself if you try to run thirty miles through the snow," Eliza said. "It's physically impossible."

Mohan smiled at her gently.

"It was precisely these winter conditions that tumo and lung-gom were designed to overcome."

"At any rate, Mohan is a yogi," Hale said. "His endurance is likely greater than the rest of us."

They waited while he considered.

"All right," he said finally. "Mohan goes to the village. The rest of us will take what steps we can to protect ourselves."

"I will need an hour to prepare," Mohan said. "Then I will leave."

He stood and went out of the kitchen. Amber also started to rise. Hale waved her back into her chair.

"There are a few things I have to say to the rest of you."

Eliza and Allan sat down, Allan taking the seat Mohan had vacated and Eliza sitting beside Lee.

"I don't want anyone left alone for an extended period, especially not at night. We're going to double up our sleeping accommodations. Amber will go in with Eliza. Allan will bunk with Lee."

"What about you?" Lee said.

Hale looked down at the dog lying beside the stove.

"I have Luther."

The dog opened its eyes sleepily at hearing its name, then pressed its chin into its paws and closed them again.

"Another thing. No one is to wander away from the house or go on solo exploring expeditions. Last night I closed the door to the cellar. This morning it was standing open. Can anyone explain that? Allan?"

"I haven't been down there since I brought up the wine," Allan said.

Hale grunted noncommittally.

"All of you, please extend your hands on the table where I can see them."

Looking questioningly at each other, they laid their hands flat on the tabletop. Eliza noticed with surprise that her fingernails were black underneath. She turned her hands over and saw faint brown stains on her palms. In the shock of seeing Mary's corpse and the letdown that followed it she had neglected to wash.

Hale reached over and took one of her hands gently. He turned it back and forth, then released it.

"There were traces of earth on Brannon's diary," he said. "Are you certain you don't remember anything of how it got into your room, Eliza?"

"I was asleep," Eliza said, confusion building inside her. "I had a bad dream."

"What kind of dream?"

"I don't know. It was dark. I was walking. I heard voices."

"Do you remember what the voices said?" Lee asked.

Eliza shook her head.

They stare at me as if I'm some kind of changeling, she thought. At last their fears and suspicions have found a focus.

"I'm going to examine the diary," Hale said. He pushed himself up from the table with both hands. "There may be something in it we can use to defend ourselves. Lee, I'm putting you in charge. I want you to arrange the rooms upstairs and see to it that Mohan gets away safely."

"All right, Professor." Lee stood and gestured to the others. "Let's go upstairs and move the beds."

Hale caught Eliza as she was leaving the kitchen.

"Would you wait a minute, Eliza? I'd like to talk to you."

"Of course."

He waited until the other three were out of hearing.

"Have you examined the internal states of the members of the group?" he said in a low voice.

"Yes."

"Any abnormalities?"

"They all seem normal," Eliza said slowly. "A bit nervous and apprehensive."

"Good." He paused. "What about my state?"

"You're normal too, as near as I can judge." She decided not to mention the increasing vacillation of his emotions since Mary's death.

He nodded with a vague relief.

"I wanted to be sure. We don't know what we're dealing with. We can't be too careful."

"Professor, you don't think I'm the one—" She did not know how to finish.

"No, of course not." Hale looked at her sadly. "The trouble is, a person can be possessed and not even realize it."

Eliza parted from him in the front hall. Hale went to the gathering room to read Brannon's diary. She climbed the stairs and helped Lee and the others dismantle the beds of Amber and Allan, then carry them piecemeal to their new locations.

Amber insisted on moving all her makeup and clothes as well. There was not enough room in Eliza's small chest of drawers for both their things, so Lee and Allan had to drag Amber's own larger bureau into Eliza's room.

"At least we'll have two heaters," Amber said, breathlessly setting her kerosene heater beside her bed.

"You could have three," Allan said mischievously. "Mary won't be using hers."

Eliza shuddered and Amber glared at him.

"Sorry," Allan mumbled. "Just a little gallows humor."

"Two should be enough," said Lee. "You can take Mohan's if you want a third."

"Where is Mohan, anyway?" Amber asked.

"Meditating." Lee looked at his watch. "He told me to call him in an hour. It's about that time."

They followed him along the corridor to Mohan's open door. Mohan sat in a full lotus position on the bare floor beside his bed, his hands folded at his groin and his thumbs touching. He was naked except for a pair of underwear briefs. Despite the fact that his heater was out, his muscular brown body was covered with a fine sheen of sweat. Steam rose in nearly invisible wisps from his shoulders.

"That's tumo," Lee said in a low voice. "It can't be started all at once. It takes time to activate."

Mohan raised his hands over his head and took a deep breath, then let it out slowly as he brought his arms to his sides. Uncoupling his legs, he stood to face them. There was a distant look in his dark eyes.

"I've made up a first-aid kit for you," Lee said, showing the yogi a small zippered case. "Aspirin. Antiseptic. Bandages. Matches. A foil emergency blanket."

"Many thanks," Mohan said with a polite smile. "But I will not need it."

"You can take it anyway, just in case," Lee argued.

"All right."

They watched him dress. He moved as though asleep, slowly drawing on knee-length socks and woolen trousers, then donning a shirt and a gold turtleneck sweater. he slid his feet into light nylon boots and absently clipped the emergency packet to his belt.

"I'm ready."

"Where's your backpack?" Eliza said.

"I need no supplies. They would only weigh me down. Once I begin I may discard this sweater—it is very heavy."

They did not argue but followed him downstairs to the back door.

"I shall return by tomorrow morning or early afternoon. Look for the boat."

With a wave he jogged across the deep snow of the lawn and into the trees. He seemed to bounce at each step as though his feet were on springs. In moments he was lost from sight.

"I hope he makes it," Amber murmured. "For his sake and ours."

They ate a late lunch from the can. It was dismal fare after Mary's cooked meals. Eliza realized that Hale had not yet washed the dishes and made a mental note to do them herself at the first opportunity. Even with the threat of death over their heads they still needed to see to the details of living.

Hale entered the kitchen as they were finishing and took a piece of hardtack and a cup of black coffee. He was strangely subdued.

"Come with me," he said, draining his cup.

Without questioning him they followed him to the gathering room. Luther was before the fire as usual. The black diary lay open on the rolltop desk. Hale carried the book to the conference table and they seated themselves around him, Allan at the end of the table on his left, Lee and Eliza across from him with their backs to the windows, Amber at the other end facing Allan.

Eliza looked at the book curiously. It was the first time she had examined it. Handwriting in a bold Italic script covered both open pages with faded brown ink. The covers were black leather. A number of slips of paper had been inserted between the pages as bookmarks.

"This is the magical diary of Daniel P. Brannon." Hale framed the book meditatively with his hands. "It covers a working conducted by his occult fraternity, the Brotherhood Of the Fiery Heart, in the year 1899. I've marked some pertinent passages. I think it would be less tedious if you take turns reading them aloud."

"Pardon me—what's a working?" asked Eliza.

"A magical operation usually requiring a series of rituals," Allan told her.

"This first excerpt is dated February the fourth."

Hale turned the book and slid it across the table to Amber, who frowned a moment at the unfamiliar Victorian handwriting, then began to read.

"'The Brotherhood has concurred with my opinion that we need a more responsive mechanism for influencing world affairs. Financial pressure, though effective in certain circumstances, is not enough. It is too liable to produce general and undirected chaos. Famines and wars do little to further our cause. Money is a social bludgeon. We need a political scalpel that will cut directly to the heart of those who seek to obstruct our goals. I have suggested that we communicate with the Lords of Light and ask that they appoint to us a special Messenger of our will that we may dispatch across the globe as the need arises. The Brotherhood has agreed to make the attempt, relying on my knowledge in such matters to guide the affair to a successful conclusion.'"

Amber slid the book back to Hale. He flipped through the pages to the next marked place.

"The following is from March twenty-third."

He passed the diary across to Lee.

"'The Lords of Light seem strangely unwilling to agree to our requests. I do not know what troubles them. Surely they realize we desire only to execute their true will upon the earth. The new social order we create will be their monument. Yet they withhold powers they formerly granted most readily, and will not come when we call them.'"

Hale took back the book and turned its pages.

"This is from April the eleventh."

Eliza accepted the book with reluctance and hesitantly read the marked passage.

"'The Lords of Light have forsaken us! On this black day the heavens were dark. The air was still. There is great consternation among the Broth-

erhood. Some openly question the direction of our
new policy. It will require strength and faith in this
hour of trial to keep the Order bound together.
May my heart burn with the unquenchable fire of
true faith, that unwavering I may serve as a model
for my brethren.'"

Suppressing her revulsion, she slid the book
back to Hale. The cover had a slick, chill feel that
reminded her of the slithering touch of a serpent.
She wondered what kind of leather had been used
to bind it.

"There's a great deal more soul searching,"
Hale said. "Then on July thirtieth the tone changes
abruptly."

He passed the book to Allan, who read his
part with theatrical gusto.

"'We are delivered from despair. Tonight one
of the Lords of Light who had not taken part in our
earlier communications addressed us directly and
agreed most graciously to fulfill our requirements.
This is a blessed day. We emerge from the valley of
shadow unbroken, our spirit strong, our will unde-
filed. We have been tested in the fires of the dark
places of the earth and our steel is true. Now I know
we will succeed! We will mould the world into our
vision of divine glory and bring the order of heaven
to flower upon the stones of human nature.'"

"The next entry is August the third," Hale
said, passing the book to Amber.

"'He has returned and laid his needs before
us. I tremble as I write, yet all the while I recognize
the necessity that compels our Lord to make so fear-

ful a set of conditions. Fire cannot be trapped in a
bottle of Air—it must be given Earth to dwell in.
Unchecked, our blazing Messenger of Death would
consume the world! We must veil his glory with our
tears, I most of all, for it is my blood that will win
him to us. Our Bright Lord exacts a heavy payment
for his service, yet we have such dire need of him.'"

"This is from October the eleventh," Hale
said. Lee accepted the diary and began to read
solemnly.

"'I have written the final letter of condolence
to the parents of the boy who was supposed to have
died of fever this past week. Poor mad child. I fancy
the letter will come as a relief to the long-suffering
couple who gave him life. His blood and the blood
of the others will provide the vitality we need to
complete our Great Work. Feigning an outbreak of
pneumonia has proved an excellent device. The
impoverished parents are more than happy to let
the Asylum bear the full expenses of burial. This
small hypocrisy will be repaid a thousand times
over when these infants are reborn in the fires of
heaven. We have set them apart in a windowless
chamber to await the fateful day of their deliver-
ance. Michael is among them. My own poor lad.'"

"I've skipped many of the details of the
preparation for the ritual," Hale said as he flipped
the pages to the next paper slip. His expression
darkened. "This is dated December the first."

Eliza accepted the book with cold hands.

"'When I see the blood flow forth from their
innocent throats I fancy I will feel myself to be a

veritable ghoul. I must steel my resolve. If I falter who will take up the knife? My strength is needed to sustain the others. There are precedents. The Apis bull and the rites of Mithra. Blood is life. My son, I will baptize you anew and you will be reborn to me. How fitting that it should happen on the dawning of the Aquarian Age. The old world gives place to the new.'"

"From December thirty-first, the date of the final ritual," Hale said, passing the book to Allan.

The spirit of mockery had deserted the theurgist. He read from the page in a quiet voice.

"'The blood flowed and drowned the struggling mad thing. He understood nothing of what was happening, and suffered little, I think. Michael, my beautiful angel, you will return to me an instrument of fiery retribution, and the earth shall roll beneath your iridescent wings.'"

Allan gave the book silently to Hale, an expression of disgust drawing down the corners of his mouth.

Hale turned a page and passed the diary to Amber.

"This is the day after—January the first in the year nineteen hundred."

"'The Messenger has come. We knelt before him and sang praises to our Bright Lord, and we were overcome by his splendor. He is beautiful, and terrible in his beauty. So darkly bright, a sword of justice to strike into the far capitals of the nations of the world! Yet he is also my son, my own dear boy. I have determined to name him Michael, see-

ing that the fiery elemental sprite that forms his
other half bears no intelligible name of its own.'"

Hale flipped through many pages, pausing
toward the end of the diary.

"I'm omitting the record of the crimes of the
Brotherhood," he said with distaste. "I haven't
counted the number of men they killed, or claim to
have killed, but it must amount to several dozen at
least, all political figures in Europe and America."

He gave the book to Lee.

"This is dated September the seventh."

"'Michael has grown increasingly unruly
over the past several weeks. I confess I am at a loss
to explain his behavior. He often refuses to manifest when we call him, and on one occasion even
came forth through the Veil unsummoned. This
cannot be allowed to continue. It is too dangerous.
There must be a reckoning between us.'"

Lee returned the diary to Hale.

"This is from November twenty-first," Hale
said, turning the pages and giving the book to Eliza.

"'It pains me to write these words. On our last
action in northern Italy, Michael killed several members of the family of our target. He would give no
reason, no explanation. When I called his conduct
vile he mocked me before the Brotherhood. He is
rapidly losing all sense of decorum. As his conduct
changes, so does his outward appearance. He has
become vulgar, even ugly, to look upon. Worse, he
will not wait for our ritual summons but presents
himself to me at the most inopportune moments.
Last night while I was at dinner! It is intolerable. The

Brotherhood has determined that he must be brought before our Bright Lord for censure.'"

"This final passage is from December the third," Hale said, passing the book for Allan to read.

"'He has defied the Lord of Light! Surely he is utterly mad. How he did so I know not—it must be his human portion with its element of free will that gives him the power. But he is mad. What have we done? In striving to raise the soul of a mad boy into an angel of glory, we have instead imbued a spirit of the flaming empyrean with all the frailties and vices of perverted humanity. I tremble to think of that which he may be capable. He must be restrained. I cannot bear to destroy him. Whatever his faults he is yet my son. I have decided to imprison him on earth, within a chamber of this very house, until I can correct the imbalance in his nature. Two C. twelve seven.'"

Hale accepted the book from Allan and shut it.

"Brannon succeeded in luring the Messenger into the black room and sealing the door shut on it, as we already know. But he died before he could deal with the problem he had created."

"Two C. twelve seven," Eliza repeated with a thoughtful frown. "Is that some sort of occult code?"

"Nothing so abstruse, I'm afraid. It's a reference to Saint Paul. Second Corinthians, chapter twelve, verse seven."

"Of course," Lee said.

Hale picked up a small book Eliza recognized as Mary's Bible and read a marked passage.

"'And lest I should be exalted above measure through the abundance of the revelations, there was given to me a thorn in the flesh, the messenger of Satan to buffet me, lest I should be exalted above measure.'"

They sat silent for several moments.

"What became of the Brotherhood?" Allan asked.

"As far as I can determine from the last few entries, it began to break up when the Messenger escaped from their control. Apparently many members were terrified of what they had ushered into the world."

"They were a bunch of cold-blooded murderers, and they were never punished," said Amber bitterly. "No wonder the spirits of the mad children still walk this ground."

"At least we know what binds the Michael-thing to this house," Eliza said.

"Madness," Lee suggested.

"No, love."

"This is just like being back at camp," Eliza said, snuggling down under her blankets.

"Not to me," said Amber through the darkness. "I had a private tent."

A gap of several feet separated the beds. Amber lay nearer the window. Lee and Allan had pushed Eliza's huge four-poster toward the door to make a space for the smaller brass bed frame.

"I wonder where Mohan is right now?" murmured Eliza.

"Wherever he is, I hope he keeps running. It's frigid outside."

"I hope he's safe. According to the diary that thing can travel anywhere."

"You mean Michael."

Eliza hissed softly.

"What's wrong?"

"Don't say it's name."

Amber giggled. There was suppressed hysteria in her voice.

"Why? Do you think it's listening? Michael, Michael, Michael."

Eliza lay silent and reached out her mind. She was startled by the level of tension that had grown in Amber since putting the room into darkness.

"If you need a pill to help you sleep," she said tentatively, "I think Allan may have something."

"Allan has enough pills to launch a moon rocket," Amber said.

"Do you want me to get up and ask him? He and Lee are probably still awake."

"Not on your life. You think I'm crazy enough to sleep with that murdering spirit wandering the halls?"

"You have to sleep sometime," Eliza reasoned.

"I'll sleep in the daylight, like Luther."

Eliza lay listening to Amber's shallow breathing. If they did not sleep, she thought, their minds would become hypersensitive, making it impossible for them to relax. This would invite disaster.

Closing her eyes, she cradled Amber's feverish emotions in her awareness and drew them close. She looked down inwardly on the feelings of the other woman. They squirmed like a child in the embrace of its mother.

I am sleepy, Eliza thought, her self impartial and detached.

There was an apprehensive wriggle from the mind of the other woman. Eliza soothed it.

I am so tired. My breath is slow and deep. So tired. My eyes close. So tired ...

Gradually the ragged hush of Amber's breathing quieted. Eliza felt her slide into the velvet darkness of sleep. Withdrawing gently, she returned to her common self with a mixed feeling of triumph and apprehension. She had only tried such a trick a few times in her life, and each time it had left her fearful of the consequences, although there had been no ill result. She lay for a time trying to relax.

Now I can't sleep, she thought.

Somewhere in the forest Mohan was running through the snow, his only guide the pale light of a quarter moon diffused through a veil of cloud. It was the same light that filtered through the window and defined the room with masses of shadow. She could see the light fixture on the ceiling, the bulk of the bureau and the smaller chest of drawers beside it. Their edges were etched by the red glow from one of the kerosene heaters that sat out of her sight below the end of the mattress. With a sigh she turned on her side and closed her eyes.

She stiffened, all her senses alert. Stillness hung in the dark around her. Somehow the room was subtly altered. Her watch arm lay beside her face, her hand tucked under her cheek. She looked at the luminous dial. It showed nearly half past three. Without meaning to she had fallen asleep for over four hours. But something had awakened her.

A soft brushing sound came from the corridor, as though a hand were sliding along the flowered paper on the wall. It came and went, came and went, always closer, until it was just outside the door. There it stopped. Eliza held her breath with her head raised from the pillow and her lips parted. She stared at the inner surface of the door and felt the pulse of her heart high in her throat. A scratching began on the other side of the oak panel.

Without thinking she shrank backwards across the four-poster and stepped to the icy floor, then climbed onto the mattress of Amber's bed. Leaning across, she put her hand over the mouth of the sleeping woman. Amber twisted her neck, eyes rolling.

"It's me," Eliza breathed into her ear. "Listen."

She removed her hand. Breath hissed between the teeth of the witch when she heard the scratching.

"Maybe it's Lee and Allan playing a joke," Eliza whispered, her mind negating the words even as she spoke them.

Amber did not reply.

The scratching began again, more insistent this time. It was as though fingers clawed at the upper half of the door, scrabbling like the hard, dry legs of a crab across the grain of the wood. They stopped, momentarily frustrated. Then they began to slid downward.

"Is it locked?" Amber breathed.

"No."

"Where's the key?"

Eliza peered through the gloom at the ornate brass knob and realized she had taken the key out of the keyhole. She tried to remember where she had put it, but her mind refused to work. In fascination she watched the knob slowly turn. It gave a soft click. The door began to open.

Amber gripped her tightly by the muscles of her shoulders and dug her fingernails into Eliza's skin, but Eliza barely noticed. Something built inside her, funnelling upward like lava in a volcano, then abruptly exploded.

"Stay out! Stay out of here!"

She tore herself away from Amber's grasp and leapt across her own bed in two bounds to hurl her body at the gaping door. The impact of her shoulder sent it slamming shut. Whatever lurked on the other side was thrown back by the sudden force. She heard it stumble against the opposite wall of the corridor.

"Get the key!" she cried to Amber, who still crouched on her bed.

"Where is it?"

"I don't know—in my purse!"

Amber began hunting about in the room in the near total darkness.

"Where did you put your purse?"

"I don't remember!"

Eliza gripped the brass doorknob in both hands and squeezed. She pressed her cheek against the wood. Her shoulder was completely numb from her neck to her elbow. She began to scream, calling out Lee's name over and over, but no answer came from outside, only the stealthy noises of a mass sliding itself against the door panel.

An awful strength turned the knob around in her perspiring fingers and began to force the door inward. Eliza braced her bare feet on the floorboards and tried to grip the smooth surface of the wood with her toes, but inexorably her feet slid back.

"Amber, help me!"

Amber left her search for the purse and ran to the door. The weight of her hands striking it once again slammed it shut. Both woman tried to grip the knob. Eliza felt Amber's fingers digging into the backs of her hands.

There was a pause, as though the intelligence on the other side was recalculating the forces opposing its entry. With an awful power the knob once again began to turn.

"We can't hold it," said Eliza.

"Where are the others?" Amber said hysterically. She began to sob.

With a sudden jerk the door opened several inches. Eliza released the now useless knob. Drawing off her wristwatch, she pressed it against the door under her two palms. She laid her forehead on the backs of her hands.

"You cannot enter," she said in a clear, trembling voice. "You are barred. You cannot enter."

She tried to extend her mind through the door, but recoiled in shock. It was like reaching into the darkness and touching ice. There was nothing to grasp hold of, only a coldness and a glittering malice.

Amber guessed what she was doing and took the silver crescent from her neck to lay it against the door.

"The Goddess watches over us," she said, struggling to keep her voice steady. "You cannot enter."

They began to chant in rhythm over and over, "You cannot enter, you cannot enter, you cannot enter." It was a children's game made deadly real and played in earnest.

The pressure against the door lessened. Bracing their feet they muscled it shut, all the while continuing to chant.

When no new force was felt for several minutes their voices died away. They stood listening. Amber looked at Eliza, who shook her head. Putting her finger to her lips, Eliza left the door and lit her lamp, then found her purse where Amber had inadvertently kicked it under the bed. She rummaged through its baggy folds and pulled out the key. Returning, she slid it quietly into the keyhole under the knob and turned it.

"Do you think it's gone?" Amber said.

"I don't know—it may be waiting."

"Can't you sense anything?"

Eliza extended her mind. She shook her head.

"Nothing. But that doesn't prove anything—it's clever."

Amber took hold of Eliza's upper arms and shook her.

"Where are the men?" she said in a low tone. "They must have heard us. Where are they?"

"Maybe it went to their rooms first. Maybe—" Eliza stopped. It was too horrible even to think about.

Gently she disengaged herself from Amber, wincing as she twisted her right arm. Her shoulder began to throb painfully. Tomorrow she would have a bruise the size of her palm. But that was the least of her worries. She slid open a drawer of the small chest and lifted out a sweater and pants.

"What are you doing?"

"Getting dressed. We may have to make a run for outside."

Silently Amber followed her example. In minutes they were fully dressed. They sat together on the side of Eliza's bed with their arms around each other and stared at the door. Time passed. Eliza looked at her watch. The crystal was cracked, but it still ran. Nearly four o'clock.

"We can't wait all night," she said at last. "The others may be hurt. Anyway, we have to know what's going on."

She stood and took up her lamp. Amber grabbed her hand.

"Are you crazy? You can't go out there."

"I have to." Eliza pulled loose. "Are you coming?"

Amber stared at her in wide-eyed terror.

"Stay here then," Eliza told her. "Lock the door after me. You'll be safe."

She turned the key and opened the door a crack, ready to slam it shut at the slightest hint of a presence in the dark beyond. Opening it wider, she extended the lamp and looked around the door jamb. The flame cast a flickering glow dimly to both ends of the corridor. It was empty. Her legs trembling, she stepped out.

Amber pressed the door shut behind her. Eliza heard the rattle and click of the lock. Slowly she advanced across the corridor toward the room that belonged to Lee and Allan. Its door stood ajar. Its interior lay in blackness. Heart hammering, she pushed the door inward with her fingertips and held the lamp before her face to look into the room. Both beds were empty, the covers disarrayed and the pillows indented. With mingled relief and dread she searched the room. It contained no horrible surprises.

Cautiously she continued on to Hale's room. It also stood open and in blackness. Neither the Professor nor the mastiff were inside. Emerging into the corridor, she looked both ways in consternation, her curiosity beginning to balance her fear.

She noticed with a shock of unease that the door at the end of the corridor stood ajar. It was the door to Mary's room. A chill draft blew out of it from the open window. With small, reluctant steps she advanced toward the door, ready to bolt at the least sign of threat. She reached the door and stood listening. The silent space beyond pulled her in.

A quick glance around assured her that nothing lurked in the shadowy corners or behind the open panel. She relaxed marginally. Mary lay as she had last seen her, head in a halo of blood. The blood had dried black. Her face was a mingled gray and white, with a waxen cast to her lips. Where before the sight had stirred revulsion in Eliza, it now moved her to pity. She drew closer.

She stopped and felt her knees buckle. An invisible hand seemed to squeeze her heart. She stared at the face of the dead woman and could not cease staring. She distinctly remembered Hale reaching down to close the eyelids of the corpse. Yet Mary's brown sightless eyes stood open.

Eliza took a breath to steady her nerves. She had heard stories of dead people twitching and opening their eyes, even sitting up in their coffins. It had to do with gases accumulating in the abdominal cavity and muscular reflexes. Steeling herself, she bent over the bed and reached to reclose the eyes of the corpse.

The dead eyes rolled and looked at her. With startling quickness a pale white hand groped for her extended wrist.

Eliza screamed and ran. Somehow she held onto the base of the lamp, although the shade tumbled away and smashed on the floor behind her. The naked flame fluttered wildly as she flew down the corridor, threatening to blow out, but it was still alight when she reached the locked door of her room. She hammered the door with her clenched fist.

"Amber, open up!"

"Eliza? What's wrong?"

"Open up, damn you, it's after me!"

There was a pause. Eliza fought down a scream. She did not dare to look behind, fearing she would lose all control and run stark raving mad.

The door opened and she tumbled through. Amber slammed and locked it. Setting the lamp down unsteadily, Eliza fell onto the bed and buried her face in her hands.

"Are they all dead?" Amber asked in a leaden voice.

"It's Mary," Eliza said with a shuddering exhalation.

"What?"

"She moved. She—that thing must be inside her."

They both whirled around as the doorknob rattled. Blows sounded on the panel.

"God, not again," said Amber.

"Eliza? Amber? Are you girls awake?" It was Lee.

Laughing with relief, Amber ran to the door and opened it. Lee entered, and behind him Allan and Hale. Luther padded in and sniffed curiously around.

Eliza could not speak. She ran to Lee and embraced him, burying her face in his shoulder. He caressed her awkwardly and stroked her hair.

"Where the hell were you?" demanded Amber.

"We heard a noise—" Allan began.

"We almost got killed, goddamn it!"

"Calm down," Hale said sharply. He led Amber to the side of the bed and made her sit. "Tell us what happened."

Amber began to describe the incidents of a short while ago. As she talked Eliza regained a measure of control. Amber reached the part about Mary and Eliza took up the story.

"Interesting," Hale said when she had finished. "Divide and conquer."

"What are you saying?" Amber demanded. "Where the hell did you go?"

"As I started to tell you before, we heard noises," Allan said. "It sounded like Mohan calling for help."

"We all heard it," said Lee. "It seemed to come from just outside the house."

"By the time we went to investigate, it had receded to the woods," Hale went on. "We followed it for a few thousand feet, but when we realized it was a trick to lead us away from Haven we came straight back."

"How could it wake you and not us?" Eliza said.

"Divide and conquer," Hale repeated. "When faced with a force of superior numbers, divide it into inferior units and overcome each separately."

"We're facing a very sophisticated being," said Lee to Eliza. "It uses our weaknesses against us. It manipulates us."

"Don't take this the wrong way," Hale said gently. "But are you certain you weren't dreaming? The whole incident may have been a psychic event."

Anger flared in Eliza. She took Hale by the arm and drew him into the corridor.

"Look at the door," she said. "Does that look like an illusion?"

Hale raised his lamp. The paint on the upper half of the panel was covered with a fine spider web of white scratches of the kind that would be made by human fingernails. Hale studied it silently. Then he and Allan went to Mary's room while Lee stayed behind with Amber and Eliza. In a few minutes the two men returned, visibly subdued.

"The fingers of the corpse are worn raw. The nails are broken," Hale said. "I've locked the door from the outside."

# 14

Eliza awoke late in the morning. After only a few hours of troubled sleep she felt exhausted rather than refreshed. Amber still lay dreaming. Not wishing to leave her alone in the room, Eliza gently touched her on the hip. The witch flinched, then relaxed as she took in her surroundings.

"I'm going to get something to eat. Are you hungry?"

Blinking sleep from her eyes, Amber stretched under the covers like a cat and thought about it.

"I believe I am. After last night, don't ask me how."

They washed and returned to their room to dress. Amber laid out half a dozen outfits across her bed, and after a few moments of internal struggle chose a red silk blouse to go with her black leather pants. She threw a knitted shawl over her shoulders for warmth, then watched Eliza put on the same drab brown sweater jacket she had worn the previous day. Eliza felt her sympathy but pretended not to notice.

Biting her full lower lip, Amber made a broad gesture of disgust at the clothes scattered across her mattress.

"Look at all this stuff. I always pack more than I need. If you see anything you like, Eliza, just grab it."

"Thanks, I will." Eliza felt her cheeks flush with mingled embarrassment and resentment. She knew Amber's intentions were kind, but hated being regarded as a charity case.

They went down to the kitchen together. Eliza cleaned the dishes from the previous two days and stacked them away. They stove was already lit. Amber opened a tin of bacon and another of sausages and made a greasy breakfast.

"I wonder where the boys are this morning," Amber said, breaking one of the hard biscuits that took the place of bread.

"Probably in the other room."

"It's so gray outside. Looks like it's going to snow again."

"Yes."

Eliza got up and went to the stove to pour herself a cup of tea.

"Eliza," Amber said slowly, "I want to apologize for the way I behaved last night."

"That's all right."

"No it's not. I locked you out. You might have been killed. I was so terrified I couldn't think straight."

"It was a natural reaction—forget it."

"Not for me it wasn't," Amber said emphatically. "I'm usually stronger than this. There's something about the atmosphere in this house that turns my spine to jelly. It's so alien—"

The thud of footsteps in the passageway drew their attention to the open kitchen door. Lee appeared and stood looking at them impassively with his cool blue eyes. He stepped forward and Eliza saw that he carried something at his side. It was a long, heavy wooden handle that swelled into a bulb at its end. The thickened part was caked with a black smear like dried current jam.

Amber dropped her fork with a clatter and slid back out of her chair away from the door. Eliza stood slowly up.

"Take it easy," Lee said, smiling weakly. "I heard voices and thought it was the Professor."

He laid the handle across the corner of the table.

"I found this under the cellar steps. It's an old pick handle. It looks like it might be the weapon that killed Mary."

They approached and studied it with mingled fascination and revulsion.

"The killer must have hidden it there."

"How did you find it?" Amber asked, looking at him guardedly. "I went down the cellar with Allan. It's as dark as a coal mine."

Lee frowned. He did not answer immediately, then looked at Eliza.

"It was funny. I decided to explore around and see if I could turn up anything useful. I didn't find anything—there's too much old junk down there. But as I was looking I started to daydream. You know how your mind goes blank when you're doing something with your hands and not really thinking of anything?"

Eliza nodded.

"When I came to I was standing beside the steps, the glow of my lamp falling on the pick handle. It was weird."

"There's something in Haven that's trying to help us," Eliza said with conviction.

"What do you mean?" said Amber.

"An intelligence—or several intelligences, I'm not sure. I think it led me to Brannon's diary the night Mary was killed."

Eliza regarded them nervously. For the first time she had dared to admit what they had been thinking—that she had been possessed the same night Mary was killed.

"Do you remember anything?" Lee asked.

"No. I only remember walking down a long slope, and voices urging me on even though they weren't speaking to me. But there was earth under my fingernails."

Amber said nothing.

"I've been thinking," Eliza continued. "The first day at Haven we drank scotch. That night Amber, Mary and I had horrible nightmares."

"So did I," Lee said. "The atmosphere of this place—"

"No, it's more than that. On Christmas we shared the wine. A few hours later I found the diary and Mary was killed."

"You think alcohol makes us more suscepti-ble to the forces working around us?" Lee said.

Eliza nodded.

"We won't have to worry on that score," Amber said dryly. "There's not a drop of hooch left in the house."

Eliza did not answer. She was thinking of Allan with his endless supply of little colored pills.

Lee levered the pick handle from the table.

"Let's take this to Hale."

They went through the freezing air of the entrance hall into the warmth of the gathering room. Hale and Allan stood over a litter of loose papers on the table, each paper covered with jotted notes and arcane symbols. Brannon's diary lay open between them.

Luther got up and rubbed his nose into Eliza's hand. She patted the dog affectionately on the shoulder.

"We were tracing the steps in the working by which Brannon evoked the Messenger of Death," Hale said, pale eyes dancing with excitement.

Allan stretched his arms behind his head and yawned.

"We've pretty well reconstructed the entire series of rituals."

"Allan's been a great help," said Hale. "I couldn't have done it without him."

Lee held up the bloody pick handle. Hale looked at it and blinked, stepping closer. Some of the academic enthusiasm faded from his features.

"What's that?"

"This is what killed Mary."

Hale took it gingerly.

"You didn't think to preserve any possible fingerprints for the police?"

"It was caked with dried mud when I found it. I beat most of it off."

Lee explained how he had found the handle.

"It's clear now what happened," Hale said, examining the blood-smeared end with distaste. "The Messenger possessed one of us while we were asleep and used that person to kill poor Mary, then hid the murder weapon in the cellar to divert suspicion and add to the confusion."

"Which of us did it use?" Amber asked. She looked at Eliza.

"We may never know," Hale said. "But whoever it was, that person has proven susceptible and therefore is still a danger."

Eliza felt the emotions of the others directed toward her and tried to turn her mind away from them. She was only partly successful.

"Why are you calling it the Messenger?" asked Lee, bending over the pages of occult diagrams. "I thought its name was Michael."

"Michael is the name Brannon used. It was a pet name, in memory of his son whose mad spirit forms part of its vitality. But the Messenger is much more than the deranged psyche of an adolescent boy. It is an unholy amalgam of a human being and a fire elemental, welded together by blood and anguish, driven by a single-minded lust to kill. It is almost unimaginably powerful."

"Elementals control vast amounts of physical energy," Allan explained. "But they lack the power of free will. Free will, simply stated, is the faculty in human beings that permits them to violate divine law. No spirit entity is able to kill. Malicious spirits use fear and confusion in an attempt to turn the powers of man against himself. Sometimes they are able to make people commit suicide, or go crazy and kill others, but spirits can't murder directly."

"I see," Eliza said. "Brannon needed the free will in the spirit of his son so that his Messenger could assassinate his enemies."

"The enemies of his grand vision of the future," Hale corrected. "Brannon was an unusual man—apparently above personal animosities. But he was that most dangerous kind of fanatic, a Utopian. He was willing to commit any crime to bring his world order into being."

"The turn of the century was a turbulent period," Lee murmured, flipping the pages of the diary. "New philosophies were threatening the old social patterns. Marxism. Nihilism. Feminism."

"Brannon was looking for a perfect world," said Allan. "The Messenger of Death was to be his instrument."

"I still don't see why he had to kill all those children," Amber said. "When I think of their little white bones I get shivers."

"Think of it this way." Hale held up his hands with the fingers spread. "In order to join two different kinds of steel you need intense heat." He laced his fingers together. "The spilling of their blood, and more importantly their terror and pain, provided a psychic forge that Brannon used to link two beings that were never intended to be linked."

Allan picked up a worn cloth-bound book from the table and showed it to Amber.

"It's not unprecedented. I've been doing some research in the Professor's library. In the Eleusinian Mysteries of ancient Greece there was a ceremony in which worshippers stood in a pit or trough while the throat of a bull, and sometimes a human being, was slit over their head. This baptism of blood was supposed to renew their life force."

"I remember a case in Hungary," Lee said. "In the sixteenth century a countess named Ersza Bathory was tried and convicted of sorcery. It turned out she had murdered hundreds of young girls and bathed in their blood to preserve her beauty."

"That's horrible," said Amber.

"And probably useless," Hale agreed. "But it does have a basis in spiritual reality. Brannon knew exactly what he was doing."

"If the Messenger is as powerful as you believe, why hasn't it killed us?" Eliza said to Hale.

"I've been giving that a lot of thought. At first I believed it was simply toying with us, but now I suspect there's something else. Its dominant part seems to be Michael, Brannon's son. We're all adults. To the confused and unstable mind of the boy we represent authority figures. Without a clear command to kill us it's uncertain how to proceed."

"Professor Hale thinks the motivating influence of the Messenger alternates between the fire elemental and the spirit of the boy," Allan said. "The elemental is wholly evil—it wants us dead. But it can't sever itself from the mind of the boy without losing its power of free will. In the night it becomes dominant and moves against us—during the day Michael's madness obstructs it."

"It's only a theory," Hale said. "We don't have much to go on."

"Does that mean we're safe during the day?" Amber asked.

"No. Merely that you're less safe at night."

"If there was just some way we could act against it," Lee said.

Hale shook his head.

"I'm hoping we won't even have to consider such a course. If we irritate it into realizing how weak we are it's liable to turn us into six smoking cinders."

"But there must be a way."

"I don't know. Frankly, this is out of my league."

Eliza was inwardly shocked at the extent to which Mary's murder had shaken Hale's nerve. Only a couple of days before he had talked brashly about destroying the entity.

"What about the Lords of Light that Brannon wrote about?" she asked.

"Spirit beings on the order of lesser gods," said Allan. "Usually they don't concern themselves in human affairs, but Brannon must have sought their aid. They are a mixed hierarchy, neither wholly good nor wholly evil. When they saw the direction the Brotherhood was going they abandoned it, all except one who Brannon called the Shining One."

"There are intriguing similarities between Brannon's Shining One and Lucifer, the fallen angel of light," Hale said to Lee. "But nothing tangible to link the two."

"Maybe it could help us fight the Messenger," Eliza said.

"No way to contact it," said Allan. "After the Messenger defied it in December of nineteen hundred, the Shining One withdrew. Brannon was unable to re-establish communication with it, although the diary indicates that he tried a number of times."

"That's it, then," Amber said, fear making her angry. "We sit and wait for it to kill us one by one."

"I hope it won't come to that," said Hale quietly. "Mohan should have reached Regret Cove by now. With luck we can expect the boat in a matter of hours."

Amber laughed.

"You don't really think he made it? Who was it you were chasing last night?"

"That may have been an audile illusion," Lee said. "The fact that you and Eliza didn't hear it suggests that it was."

They sat talking in a desultory fashion for several hours. Every few minutes one or the other would go to the windows and look out across the ruffled gray sea. At noon they broke for lunch, and in the afternoon they returned to the gathering room, more subdued than they had ever been. The warm, stuffy air was thick with unacknowledged tension.

Eliza found herself getting one of her bad headaches. It throbbed between her temples more intensely when she rubbed them. She clenched her fists and suppressed the urge to scream. Instead she closed her eyes and laid her head against the high back of the couch.

"What's wrong?" Lee asked. He had been watching her.

"Nothing—just a headache."

"I'll get you an aspirin."

"They don't do any good."

He went to the emergency case and took out two aspirin from their tin box, then poured ginger ale from a can into a crystal goblet left over from the wine.

"Here, try them anyway."

She swallowed the pills and drank a bit of the ginger ale, then stretched herself out on the couch on her shoulder and stared at the fire.

This was what she had feared most, even before coming to Haven. She had grown to know the others too well. Her mind was attuned to their emotional wavelengths. Like a sensitive radio receiver it focused and magnified their feelings unendurably. They were too close to block out. She was rapidly losing control. Their fear and suspicion and horror and sense of helpless frustration flooded in and overwhelmed her own weaker feelings, threatening to drown her inner identity.

Forcing down a shudder, she sat up. Nausea rocked between her head and stomach.

"Professor Hale, I'm going for a walk. I need to be alone."

She felt his sympathetic concern like the blast from a loudspeaker.

"I understand. Do you want one of us to walk behind you?"

"No—no. I want to be by myself."

Lee watched her. Only his emotions were stable. They reached out to her warmly. She averted her eyes and stood up.

"You should be safe enough," Hale said, as much to himself as to Eliza. "Nothing's happened outside except at the quarry. Stay out of the woods and keep within sight of the house."

"I will."

She put on her camel coat, red mittens and beret in the kitchen and stepped out the back door. The air was mild and the wind low. Large flakes of snow like crystal parachutes spun and fell from the slate sky. The heavy cover of ground snow compressed silently under her boots. As she walked around the side of the house little cones of snow caked on her toes and flipped through the air in front of her when she brought her feet forward.

Descending to the edge of the front lawn, she turned and made her way toward the stony point with the pebble beach below her on her left. The level house grounds gave way to a rough margin of bush and twisted wild grasses, their nodding brown tips exposed between the drifts. The great axe head of black granite thrust in an angled ridge far out from the shore. No spruce grew on its wind-blow crest. At its edge a ragged line of turf showed where the cover of snow had slid and fallen into the sea. It was beside this that Eliza walked, placing her feet in the snow with care to keep from stumbling.

The wind blew stronger above the level of the trees. When she turned her gaze across the crawl-ing waves of the gray ocean, the snow slanted into her eyes and blinded her. She hunched her shoul-der, looking back the way she had come. Haven lay spread out below. She could see the window of the gathering room in the east wing, and wondered if anyone was watching her at that moment, high on this naked arm of rock with the sky behind her.

She stood breathing in her freedom, almost happy, so great was the release of her emotions. Nothing assailed her but the brush of snowflakes against her cheek, the scent of salt spray, and the rustle of the waves on the rocks below. The snow lying against her boots began to chill her toes. She took a step and shook it off.

If only it could be this way always, she thought. Silent and alone. Even in crowded cities other people could withdraw and be with their pri-vate thoughts. How she envied them. To look upon others and not know what they were feeling. What bliss that would be. Not to have to guard her mind from emotion. Not to have to erect a wall around her heart.

It was time to return. She hesitated, unwilling to leave the protective sanctuary she had found. At last she began placing her feet in the holes she had made in the virgin snow. It should have been easier. The way back was downhill with the wind behind. But to Eliza it seemed more laborious than the climb. Her foot slipped and she had a dizzy look at the sea close below her right hand. Deliberately she bent her steps farther away from the edge.

Wrapped in her own thoughts, it was a while before she noticed the solitary figure walking toward her from the line of trees at the base of the point. She wiped her welling tears on her mitten and narrowed her eyes, then recognized Mohan by his gold turtleneck sweater. It was so covered with snowflakes that distance made its color indistinct.

Her heart began to thud. He made no sign of recognition but walked with a measured pace toward her in a line that would intersect her curving path back to Haven. She could not avoid him. Behind her lay the narrowing crest of the point and on either side the sea. Before her was the open margin between the shore and the forest. She continued to walk at a natural pace.

Reaching out her perceptions, she probed him cautiously. He was calm inside, neither pleased nor regretful at seeing her. But there was something unnatural about his emotions. They felt stiffly artificial. Perhaps, she thought, exposure to the wilderness has induced some psychic trauma. He stopped and waited for her. She approached within six feet and also stopped.

"We thought you'd be in the village by now," she said quietly. "What happened?"

"I do not quite know." His voice was husky. He frowned. "Something took hold of my mind. I remember running and shouting."

"How did you get back to Haven?"

"I do not know. It is puzzling."

Eliza relaxed slightly. He had obviously suffered the same temporary madness that had seized Luther.

"Come back to the house. You must be freezing."

"I'm not cold. But I am very hungry."

She walked past him and he took up a pace behind her.

"The others will be disappointed," she said. "They were counting on you rescuing them."

"Maybe I will try again."

"It'll have to wait until after this snow. If much more falls it could make traveling in the woods impossible."

They began descending a difficult section of the rocks where walking was uneven and made treacherous by hidden pockets of ice. Eliza crouched and put her hand on a boulder to steady herself.

"Let me help you," Mohan said from behind.

He took her arm. A tightening in his fingers made her turn. She cried out and struggled to free herself. Red fury blazed from his eyes. His lips drew back from his barred teeth in a snarl. Before she could brace her feet or defend herself he struck her brutally on the side of the head with his clenched fist.

For a moment she spun free in space. The
earth and sky turned a cartwheel. She saw Mohan
leaning out with his arms spread crabwise, and
Haven tumbling on its head. Then the rounded sea-
worn boulders on the beach rose up to catch her.

# 15

Water from melting snowflakes cooled the inner edges of her eyelids. Eliza blinked and saw the snow whirling toward her out of a steely sky. Every so often a flake landed directly in one of her eyes, making her wink it away.

Pain flooded through her body but she could not determine its point of origin. Her mind was strangely detached. She gradually realized that she was moving. Soft voices murmured around her. She focused her eyes and saw the backs of Hale and Amber. Lee and Allan were also there leaning over her, concern in their faces.

Her hand slid across her hip and banged into something hard and round. She felt it and recognized a doorknob.

I'm being carried on a door, she thought wonderingly. Isn't it dead people they carry on doors? She closed her eyes.

When she opened them it was warmer. Lifting her head, she looked around. She was in the gathering room stretched out on the conference table with a blanket over her and a pillow under her head. The others stood looking down at her. Amber wiped her forehead with a cool cloth.

"She's coming around," Amber said.

"Is she in shock?" asked Lee.

"I don't think so," Hale said. "Her color's good. But I'm not a medical doctor. We'd better keep her warm."

"I was with Mohan," Eliza muttered, surprised to find her mouth dry as cotton. "He pushed me."

"Hush," said Amber. "We know. We saw it from the window."

"I'm thirsty—"

Amber lifted Eliza's head and gave her a sip of water from a cup she had ready on a chair beside her.

"Wiggle your toes," Hale said.

Eliza did as directed.

"Now your fingers."

A stab of pain lanced up her left arm when she moved her fingers.

"My arm hurts."

"We think it's broken." Lee took her other hand between his and rubbed its back. "We were trying to decide how to fix it."

"It has to be set," Hale said. "We'll break one of these wooden chairs and make splints from the rungs. Amber can tear a bed sheet up for bandages."

"Do you know how to set a broken arm?" Allan asked.

Hale pulled on his white beard, a worried expression on his face as he studied Eliza.

"I've had a little emergency training, but I've never set a bone."

"Then we're liable to do more harm than good."

"We can't leave it like this for a week," Hale said in irritation. "Unless someone wants to volunteer to walk to the village."

"I'll try it," said Lee.

"No, sorry Lee," Hale said in a more subdued tone. "With that madman out there and the way the snow's coming down, it's out of the question."

"Then we set it," Allan said. "How do we start?"

Hale gently lifted Eliza's left arm from the table. She saw that her forearm was swollen and irregular on one side. She realized that her coat and sweater were off, but had no recollection of them being removed. Someone had rolled the loose sleeve of her shirt up above her elbow.

"The bones have to be pulled apart and realigned." Hale probed the swelling gently. "It's likely to be painful."

"I can give her something to make her sleep," Allan offered.

"No, no drugs." Eliza struggled to sit up and Amber held her down.

She had a vision of herself lying helplessly unconscious while a shadowy menace approached. Whatever the pain she wanted her wits about her.

"I understand," Hale said soothingly. "We won't knock you out, Eliza. Anyway, not with drugs."

He glanced at Amber and Allan.

"Get the splints and bandages."

They left Eliza's circle of vision. She heard splintering noises, but her mind was too confused to identify them or even to make her turn her head. Lee bent over her.

"You trust me, Eliza," he said. It was both a statement and a question.

Of course, she thought, and was not certain if she had said it aloud.

"Look into my right eye."

He took her face in his two hands and began to brush her forehead and the bones of her cheeks.

"Listen to my voice. Relax. Try to make your mind receptive. Think of yourself as a still pool of water, and my words as drops falling into the pool and vanishing. You can feel my hands on your face, but soon you won't feel them. Your face will become numb and then your eyes will close, but you'll still hear my voice ..."

She felt herself resisting automatically as the ordinary defensive screens went up in her mind. Gathering her resources, she forced herself to open up to him while she listened to his quiet words. Soon she saw only his face, then only his blue eye. It seemed to grow and change, streaming his words in the form of tiny crystal tears into her emptiness. A void neither dark nor light surrounded her and she floated free.

"She's back," said a childish voice.

"She hears," said a second.

"But will she remember?" a third asked.

"She must—we'll show her," the first said.

"She forgot before," the third reminded.

"That was different," said the first voice. "She was shielding herself from us."

"It will find out and punish us," the third voice said fearfully.

"No. It's busy outside, in the woods," said the first.

"Hurry, then," said the second.

"Hurry, hurry, hurry."

Eliza walked along a shadowy corridor. On either side doors stood open. People rushed in and out of the rooms in a brisk manner, passing near her without a glance as though she were invisible. They wore strange costumes which she recognized as Victorian clothes. Many were in servant uniforms, the maids with hair drawn up in the back and frilly white aprons on black dresses and button shoes, the menservants in starched white collars and black suits, their silver buckles gleaming, their hair parted in the middle and their white gloves immaculate.

Although they chatted to each other as they met in the corridor Eliza could not hear their voices. Haven itself was subtly transformed. The walls were covered in ornately patterned paper and the floors warmed by cosy oriental rugs. Fires flickered silently in all the rooms. Candles burned in chandeliers overhead, but their light did not dispel the grayness of the scene.

She emerged into the entrance hall. A group of gentlemen and ladies stood by the door talking while servants bustled around them moving trunks and other luggage. Where the hotel reception desk had been rested two matching rollback ottomans and a low marble table. Oil paintings hung on the walls. A large fire blazed noiselessly in the fireplace.

One of the gentlemen turned away from the group to relight his cigar with a wooden match. He glanced up. With a slight interior shock Eliza recognized Daniel P. Brannon. He did not seem to notice her but his charcoal eyes dwelt meditatively on the hearth where she stood transfixed. He turned back to the lady he had been speaking with, who made some remark that caused him to laugh.

Eliza continued across the hall and stole swiftly along the paneled back passage to the plain cellar door opposite the entrance to the kitchen. It opened before her and she descended into the denser gloom. Although there were no lights burning and no windows, somehow she could still find her way. The walls and ceiling, even the earthen floor, seemed to radiate a soft light. It was the first time she had been in the cellar, but it felt oddly familiar.

The vast mass of Haven pressed unseen upon the low ceiling. Thick stone pillars rose at intervals from the black earth. Stone walls divided the dark space into rooms and corridors. She moved past a massive iron machine she recognized in a detached way as a steam furnace. A wooden coal bin filled with small bits of coat stood beside it. Through a grate in the cast iron door of the furnace fire burned with a dull red glow. She turned left and continued along a brick walkway laid down in the middle of the passage in the earthen floor.

Somewhere under the west wing she stopped. This part of the cellar had been set aside for storing wine. The floor was made of flat stones and swept relatively clean. Wooden racks held dusty bottles in their diamond-shaped compartments. Several barrels were stacked against a wall. At the back of the wine room was a heavy wooden door made of rough-sawn planks fastened together with black iron straps. She felt herself attracted to it. She touched the door and it opened soundlessly.

Beyond lay a root cellar filled with bins of vegetables, their ends projecting out of the sawdust packing. She recognized potatoes and beets. A rough rack on the wall held jars and crockery. But Eliza's attention was drawn to an undistinguished spot on the bare earth floor. Kneeling, she began to rake at the dry black loam with her fingers, scooping it toward her. Strangely her left arm was unbroken and free of pain. Even as the thought fluttered past her consciousness it was blown away.

She felt a rough fabric under her fingers and began to pull on it. Try as she might, it would not come out of the hole. She braced her feet and yanked it from side to side, gritting her teeth at the sudden lance of pain in her arm. For some reason it was vital that she get the canvas sack out of the earth. There was something important in it, something she must show the others.

"We are losing her," the first voice said.

"No matter," sighed the second. "She has seen. She will remember."

Eliza opened her eyes. She immediately became aware of the deep throbbing in her left arm. She lifted it and saw that it was swathed in a thick white bandage from the elbow to the wrist.

"Don't move it," Amber said beside her. "Let it heal."

Eliza looked around and realized she was in her bed in their upstairs room. Blankets covered her to the chin. Both her arms lay on top of them. She felt the cotton sheet against the skin of her bare back. Someone had stripped her to her bra and panties and put on her pajama bottoms, all without her knowing it.

A small table had been brought in and placed between the two beds. On its top stood a pitcher of water and a glass beside a flat metal box.

"Aspirin," Amber said, following her eyes. "I took them from the first-aid kit."

"Thanks."

Amber smiled and touched her arm protectively.

"You need them more than we do—I don't know how you can stand it."

"It's not so bad."

"There's a trick witches use to control pain," Amber said hesitantly. "I'll teach it to you, if you like. You may need it when the aspirin run out."

"Show me."

Amber looked around the room, then pointed at an oil lamp that rested on top of her bureau.

"See that lamp over there?"

Eliza nodded.

"I want you to reach out to it with your mind. Try to feel its smoothness and shape. Try to see it from all sides at once."

Eliza sent an imaginary hand out to caress the glass base of the lamp. She felt the curves of its shade and the damp, furry texture of it wick.

"Continue to hold the lamp in your mind. Now at the same time become conscious of the pain in your arm. Can you do that?"

"I think so."

"Good. This next part is tricky. The pain is no longer in your arm, it's inside the base of the lamp. Feel it throbbing and aching inside the lamp. Let there be no doubt in your mind. Just feel it in the lamp. It's no good trying to push it there—you must feel it there already."

The glass of the lamp surrounds my pain, Eliza thought. It is aching inside the glass, aching under the cool oil. For a moment she actually felt the coolness against the hot skin of her forearm under its bandage.

"I feel it."

"This next part is easy. Disengage your mind from the lamp, but leave your pain behind inside it. Hold to the certain conviction that your pain is over there on the bureau and no longer inside your body. Don't force it, just understand that it's the truth. The pain can't be in two places at once. You left it inside the lamp, so its not inside you."

"That's amazing," Eliza said, blinking at Amber.

She could feel her pain throbbing inside the lamp. But since the lamp was detached from her body the pain no longer had any power to hurt her. It was like the pain inside someone else.

Amber smiled.

"You're a quick study. It took me weeks to learn that trick."

She busied herself with something on the table.

"What's that?" Eliza asked.

"I've made a sling so you can walk around when you feel better. I'll put it on if you like."

Eliza nodded and lay back on the pillow with her eyes closed. She felt Amber's fingers fussing over her arm and shoulder like the fluttering wings of a bird. Images stirred in her interior darkness. She remembered a bizarre dream. She had been digging in the cellar and had unearthed a sack, but it would not come out of the hole. And there had been maids in Victorian uniforms. And Daniel P. Brannon had looked at her.

As she thought about the dream it returned with greater intensity. She remembered strangely familiar voices but could not think what they had said. Did it have any significance, she wondered, or was it only the result of her injury and Lee's soothing words.

"How are you?"

She opened her eyes. Lee stood in the doorway. He came in and sat on the side of the bed opposite Amber.

"What did you do to me?" she asked with mild reproach.

"Hypnosis. I put you in a light trance so you wouldn't feel the pain when we reset your arm."

"How did it go?"

"Like a charm. I felt the bones snap back into place."

Amber winced.

"Sorry Amber," Lee said. He smiled at Eliza. "You should be the squeamish one."

"I would be, if I let myself think about it."

Lee took her right hand in his and squeezed it encouragingly.

"Do you remember anything about it—I mean before Mohan pushed you?"

"He seemed normal enough," she said, shuddering. "I talked to him. He was confused and sort of vague. I thought the same thing that happened to Luther had happened to him."

"We may have been wrong about the dog," Lee said.

"How do you mean?"

"I don't think Luther was ever taken over. I think he just saw something through the window and ran wild for a time."

"Speaking of which," said Amber, "You'll be glad to know that the boys moved Mary out of the house while you were asleep."

"Hale thought it would be better," Lee said. "We put her in the stable wrapped in a blanket, and locked the door."

"I'm glad," said Eliza, settling back into the pillow.

It was a relief to know that the corpse was no longer just a few doors down the corridor. Irrationally she felt safer, even though she knew they were all still in grave danger.

"Allan and Hale are closing the storm shutters," Lee went on. "The entire ground floor will be sealed, just in case Mohan comes back in the night."

She turned her face to the window. Snow was still falling, thicker now through the gathering twilight.

"He may die out there."

"I know. But there's nothing we can do. We tried calling him. He doesn't answer."

Persistently, like a mental fly buzzing past her ear, the memory of the dream returned. She decided to mention it to Lee for what it might be worth.

"While I was hypnotized I had the strangest dream—"

Distant barks and shouting voices stopped her. They listened for several seconds. A howl rose and trailed away mournfully. It was an eerie sound, unlike any Eliza had ever heard. The barking began again and changed to savage growls. There were more shouts, followed by a chilling series of animal screams.

Lee released her hand and ran from the room without a word.

Amber hurried around the foot of the bed after him.

"Amber, don't leave me!"

"You'll be all right," Amber said quickly from the door. "The others may need my help."

Eliza lay alone with all her senses alert, listening to the beating of her own heart. There was utter silence throughout the house. When she could no longer stand the waiting she pulled herself out of bed, cradled her arm close to her chest and wrapped a blanket about her shoulders with her good hand. She went into the corridor and made her way toward the front stairs, the floorboards creaking under her bare feet.

They were gathered inside the front door. Pale light filtered through the unshuttered upper windows of the hall. Eliza stopped halfway down the marble staircase. Hale sat on the flagstones with his back against the door, blood streaming down his face from a wound on his scalp. Amber was vainly trying to staunch the bleeding with his handkerchief, which had turned a bright scarlet. Allan stood crookedly supported by Lee. His navy pea jacket was rent open at the shoulder as though by the claws of some animal.

"We finished the shutters and were taking one last look around," Allan said, his voice strained. "He attacked without warning. I don't know where he came from. He knocked me down and tore at the Professor. I think he would have killed us both if it hadn't been for Luther."

"Where is Luther?" Eliza said.

She descended to the floor of the hall.

"Dead," Lee said quietly. "Mohan killed him—broke his back."

"We only barely managed to get the door locked against him," Allan said. "He's incredibly strong. He's not a man anymore, he's something else."

A bestial scream of fury cut through the exterior wall. Some great mass slammed against the front door and made the oak panel flex on its iron hinges. They listened silently. The assault was not repeated.

"He was a good dog," Hale muttered to himself, head cradled in his hands.

# 16

As darkness fell Hale had several mattresses and all the blankets brought down to the gathering room. His voice was unnaturally subdued as he gave the order to move the Christmas tree to an empty chamber where it would be out of the way. They settled into a state of siege. Lamps were kept burning throughout night. The men took shifts remaining awake while the rest tried to sleep.

Mohan continued to test the doors and shutters as he restlessly circled the house in the darkness. Eliza heard him scratching and banging in the still, early morning hours. At intervals a sudden noise would wake her, and she would lie frightened and exhausted but unable to close her eyes until fatigue overcame her.

The worst of it was when he spoke. He called to each of them by name and begged them to let him inside, saying that he was cold and hungry. At times his voice was pitiful, at other times angry. Now and then it trailed into guttural animal sounds, and the groaning creak of the window shutters attested to the force applied against them.

But the shutters had been made when Haven was still a summer home, and had been designed to withstand not only the Atlantic storms but the casual attacks of vandals. They held.

Dawn brought no ray of light into the stuffy room and no relief from the tension. The kerosene lamps and the dull embers of the fire gave off a sooty glow that strained their eyes and wore their tempers raw. The intermittent banging and scratching outside kept their nerves always on edge. While it went on it occupied their full awareness. When it stopped the waiting for it to begin aborted attempts at conversation.

Eliza began to feel like a trapped beast. The dark, shuttered room was an outward reflection of her state of mind. Her thoughts raced like a small animal on a treadmill endlessly round and round, further inflamed by a low fever caused by the healing of her broken arm. Throughout the sunless day and all through the still, tense hours of the night the scraping continued without let.

On the second day of waiting Eliza's tight-lipped self-control began to unravel.

"We can't just leave him out there to die," she said in a loud voice.

The scraping at the shutters had ceased for several minutes. They were silently waiting for it to resume.

"What do you suggest?" Amber said. "That we let him in to take another crack at us?"

"At least we could put out food and blankets."

"He's got food."

"What do you mean?"

Amber rattled nervously in her purse and tapped out a cigarette. Stress had driven her back to her old habit. She worked her lighter several times before it flamed.

"I mean the dog. I saw it from upstairs. Its underside is all open and bloody."

Eliza stood and paced around the table to listen at the window for a moment. Silence.

"Maybe we could tie him up. Lee?"

Lee shook his head, his expression sympathetic.

"That's what the Messenger is waiting for. It's much stronger now than it was two days ago."

She had expected at least moral support. His denial hurt her.

"You talk about Mohan as though he were already dead," she said accusingly.

"Damn it, Eliza, wake up," Amber said. "It's him or us."

"I say it's murder." She appealed to Hale, who sat at the desk not looking at them, his bandaged head propped in his hand. "What do you suppose the police will say when they discover what we've done? They'll say we scared ourselves silly, then locked Mohan out and let him freeze to death."

"Justifying our actions is the least of our worries," Hale said wearily.

"I see," Eliza said. "You're all willing to let this bogey man, this shadow, turn us into animals."

They looked at her unspeaking.

"That's what we are, isn't it? Apes hiding in a cave."

Allan stood up from the couch and stretched, then went to the table. He lifted a leg over its corner and sat with his hands folded on his thigh.

"In some measure I agree with Eliza," he said in a quiet voice. "I've been doing a lot of thinking these past few days. We were wrong to let the Messenger set its own terms. We're playing its game. It's using our weaknesses against us."

"Agreed." Lee pulled out a chair and sat beside him. "But what can we do? We have no weapons to fight it."

"We have to wait," Hale said in irritation. "Today's the twenty-ninth. The boat will be here on the second."

Amber let out a brief shrill laugh.

"It's not going to let us get on the boat. It's biding its time until it's strong enough to kill us."

"Shut up," Allan told her. "Professor, I'm sorry but I can't sit and do nothing. I'm going to try to fight it."

"No," Hale said sharply. "After the New Year its power will dissipate. We only have to hold out two more days."

"That's not good enough," Allan said.

"I'll decide what's good enough!" Hale stood up, the knuckles of his hand white where he gripped the back of his chair. "This isn't a democracy, this is a field expedition and I'm running it. You'll do what I say."

"Stop fighting, you fools," Eliza said. "Can't you see that's what it wants?"

The tension felt like sandpaper scraping along her nerves. She could no longer defend herself. It attacked her from every direction at once. Her head throbbed like a drum.

Amber got up.

"I'm going upstairs where there's some daylight," she said, and stalked from the room.

Hale took a breath and seemed to collect himself.

"Follow her, will you Allan? I don't want anyone left alone. We'll talk later."

Allan nodded and went after Amber.

The remaining three looked at each other, the silence thickening between them. At the shutter behind Eliza the soft scratching began again.

"I have to get out," Eliza said. She took up a lamp. "I'll check the lock on the back door—it will give me something to do."

The door at the end of the rear passage was secure. Eliza suppressed the impulse to unlock and open it just for a moment to breathe the fresh icy air. The dark interior of the house stifled her. She went into the kitchen, where the belly of the iron stove cast a dull red glow across the tiles.

"Mind if I join you?"

Lee came into the kitchen and set his lamp next to hers on the table. His inner stillness soothed her despite her lingering resentment. He put his hand on the side of her neck. She pulled away and toyed nervously with a button on her sweater.

"I suppose Hale sent you—he's like a mother hen."

"How's the arm?" he asked, ignoring her remark.

"Better. It doesn't hurt so much. It's starting to itch."

"Eliza—"

She faced him.

"Why didn't you back me up, Lee? I thought I could count on you."

"You know you can. but I have to think for everyone."

"You're willing to let Mohan die in the snow."

He took her shoulders in his hands.

"Mohan is like a rabid wolf. We'd have to kill him before we could take him."

"Maybe that would be kinder."

"Maybe. But then that thing would possess someone else."

He leaned close. She embraced him with her good arm, protecting the other in its sling with her upper body. They kissed. She broke the contact of their lips, breathing faster. The hardness of his body made her knees weak. Her back curved like a bow over his supporting hand.

"Let's find a room where we can be alone," Lee murmured into her hair.

"No. They'll come looking for us."

"Let them look."

She pulled away and laughed.

"I thought you had to think for everyone."

"I wasn't talking about thinking."

She stepped to the side and put the kitchen table between them.

"Are you going to help Allan?"

His face became more serious.

"I think so. Allan's right, we have to take the risk and confront it. I just wish we had a weapon."

"What weapon could possibly hurt it? It doesn't even have a body."

"A symbol of some kind." His blue eyes flashed. "On the subtle planes of being symbols are tangible. They can maim and kill."

"It's hard to know where illusion ends and reality begins."

"Sometimes it is," he agreed. "The lives of men are the dreams of God."

"I had a funny dream when you hypnotized me," Eliza said thoughtfully. "I forgot about it in all the excitement."

She told him about walking through the Victorian edition of Haven, and about seeing Brannon, and digging in the cellar.

"There were voices that sounded weirdly familiar, though I can't think where I've heard them before."

"What sort of voices?" Lee asked with mounting interest.

"Childlike, but sort of old at the same time. Three of them. They led me somehow."

"Were they the voices you heard in your other dream?"

"Maybe—I'm not sure."

Lee paced in front of the stove and stood with his hands on his hips.

"I didn't think it was important," Eliza said. "It was only a dream."

"Dreams are uncommon in hypnotic sleep," he said, turning to her. "It may have been a psychic message from spirit entities trying to help us."

"Or a trick."

"Yes. There's one way to find out. Come on."

He grabbed his lamp up from the table and drew her after him by the hand.

"Where are we going?"

"The cellar."

"Wait—I need a light."

Impatiently he paused while she took up her lamp. They crossed the chill back passage to the cellar entrance. Lee pulled the plank door open and stepped into the darkness. Eliza followed. An earthy puff of moist, warmer air rose to engulf them.

It was both the same and different from her dream. The walls were in the places she remembered, and the dark mass of the furnace. The thin ribbon of bricks that formed the walkway in the dirt floor still ran down the middle of the main passage. But cobwebs that had not been in her dream hung thick in every corner and trailed from the beams of the low ceiling to brush her face and tangle in her hair. She held her lamp up to ward them off, and they burst into brief strings of sparks on contact with the hot shade.

"Careful," Lee said. "You'll set the place on fire."

"I'm not getting cobwebs in my mouth," she said indignantly. "You've got two hands—I haven't."

They passed into the wine cellar. It was as Eliza remembered it from her dream, but the racks were empty. One rack had fallen onto the flagstone floor and splintered. The small door at the other end of the chamber stood crooked in its frame. When Lee pulled on its latch it fell out toward him in a shower of dust and rusty flakes of iron. The hinges had disintegrated in the damp air.

Eliza followed Lee into the root cellar. The preserve shelves were bare. The wooden bins held no produce. A few empty burlap sacks littered the earth floor like the pelts of dead animals.

"I remember walking over here," she said half to herself. "And kneeling down."

Lee dropped to his knees and held his lamp near the floor.

"It's been dug," he said with excitement. "Look, the earth's piled up."

Eliza crouched and brushed at the granular black soil with confusion.

"It can't be. Anyway, I'm sure I didn't do it— I've never been down here."

"Are you positive?"

"Yes. Only in the dream."

Lee picked up a piece of yellow-orange paper. It showed a rectangular pattern of creases. The edges were stuck together with red wax. It had been torn open. He held it close to the lamp and examined its texture, then smelled it.

"Oilskin," he said. "It was used to wrap something."

"Brannon's diary," she said with sudden realization.

"Maybe. The diary had black earth clinging to it but was undamaged, meaning it hadn't been exposed to any damp."

She studied his face. The upward-slanting lamplight gave it a sinister cast. I must look the same to him, she thought.

"You think I was the one who found Brannon's magic book."

"You're the most likely candidate. It couldn't have been Mohan, not if he killed Mary, and the book was in your room."

"But I don't remember," she said in exasperation.

"You were unconscious. Something in this house guided you."

She stood up with her lamp.

"Then the dream doesn't mean anything. I was only remembering what I did before."

"In your dream you were pulling a sack. This isn't a sack," he said, holding up the oilskin.

"No, but you know how dreams are. They're always confusing one thing with another."

He got up and began casting around the chamber with his head bent low. She followed him into the wine cellar.

"What are you looking for?"

"Something to dig with."

Stepping inside the fallen wine rack, he lifted his heel and brought it down on one of the oak cross members. The strap of wood splintered with a loud crash. Lee twisted it loose from the nail holding it to the frame and carried the stick into the root cellar. he began to dig in the depression of the floor. Eliza put her lamp where it would cast the best light and stood watching.

When he had gone down two feet he paused and wiped his head with his sleeve, grinning up at her. Dirt on the cuff of his denim shirt left a black streak on his brow.

"If there's anything here, it's deep," he said.

"Give it up, Lee. You're getting filthy."

"I'll change clothes after we're finished."

Stubbornly he went back to work. The hole was nearly a yard below the level of the floor before he struck something hard. He brushed the dirt aside with his hands and tapped the black surface below experimentally with his stick. It thudded with a hollow sound.

Eliza leaned over the hole to look.

"That's not what I saw in my dream."

"Maybe this is the treasure Biddingford was looking for," he grunted as he tugged at the exposed wooden corner.

"It's some sort of trunk," said Eliza.

In a few moments its outline was free of soil. It took all of Lee's strength to lift it straight out of the hole, but once clear of the clinging sides of earth it proved to weigh little.

"No lock," Lee said. "Can't contain anything too valuable."

He loosened the clasp. Eliza drew back nervously. The square wooden lid squeaked open.

"Here's your sack," Lee said.

Inside the trunk was a gray bundle sewn around the edges with thick twine. Lee pulled it out and set it on the ground.

"Sailcloth," he murmured.

The rotten stitches resisted his strenuous efforts to part them for several moments. Abruptly they broke. A cascade of white bones tumbled to the floor. A skull rolled toward Eliza. She shrank away from its touch.

"More bones," Lee said. "Another child by the look of them. This place must be a regular cemetery."

With a slight grimace of disgust he piled the bones back into the canvas sack and held it closed with his fingers.

"All that work for nothing," Eliza said, glancing nervously behind her.

"Not necessarily. Ask yourself why all the other skeletons are in the quarry, and this one is here buried inside a sack and a trunk."

She shrugged. "It was buried at a different time, I guess."

"But why not at the quarry with the rest?"

"By a different person, then."

"Possible, but unlikely."

"Somehow this body was different from the others?"

"That's it." He rattled the bones. "The corpses of the other children were treated with contempt. This one was accorded respect. The others were piled together under a few stones. This was interred—and not the whole body. These bones were carefully cleaned of flesh and sewn into this sack, then buried in the trunk. This is a legitimate grave."

She stared at him.

"Michael Brannon," she said softly.

He nodded.

"It would explain why this place was important enough for you to dream about, and why the diary was put here long after the original burial."

"I assumed Michael's bones were in the quarry with the rest."

"We all did," Lee said. "But remember, Brannon loved his son."

"Even if this is Michael's grave, what good does it do us?"

Lee stood and gripped her elbows with excitement. She winced as the sudden pressure jarred her injured arm but he did not notice.

"This is the weapon we've been looking for," he said intensely. "Through these remains we can work against the human side of the Messenger."

Eliza looked around at the shadows apprehensively. She did not like to hear the name of the thing spoken aloud. It seemed too much like calling the evil toward them.

"We'd better get upstairs," she said. "Hale probably has Amber and Allan tearing the house apart looking for us."

They took up the lamps and retraced their path toward the cellar steps. Lee went in front with the canvas bundle of bones. They passed the brooding bulk of the old furnace. Eliza's spirits began to lift.

Without warning both lamps went out.

"Lee—?"

"Eliza, don't move. I'll get out my lighter."

The dark was absolute. Never had Eliza experienced such total blackness. The walls of earth and stone pressed upon her and muffled up her nervous words. She began to gasp. Her breaths became louder and louder until they roared in her ears with hurricane velocity. Even the air seemed to shift and whirl about her. Sly fingers brushed her neck and face. She reached blindly out and stumbled with dizzy steps through the void, her free arm beating at the swirling air.

She shouted as loudly as she could but the rising noise of the wind drowned her words. Dimly, like the echo of her own thoughts, she heard an answer. The thunderous rushing increased until it was a great cataract of sound, and even the echo was lost in seamless space.

Is it outside or inside my mind? she wondered. A confused cacophony of gibbering voices mocked her. Inside and outside were one. The margin formed by her skin dissolved and she swayed and clawed vainly with her single arm for support,

uncertain whether she stood or fell endlessly
through some bottomless crevasse.

Am I going mad? Is this what Mohan has been
feeling? If I'm possessed, what is my body doing?

Somewhere nearby Lee was alone with her in
the darkness. Concern for him focused her chaotic
thoughts. With a supreme act of will she forced
herself to disengage her attention from her over-
loaded senses. Instead she fixed on the color of
Lee's emotions. Faintly through the blizzard of
background noise she sensed him. He was concerned and apprehensive for something apart from
himself. He was worried about her, she realized.
Warmth flowed through her and gave her strength.

Forcing her nerveless legs to work, she
groped blindly toward the source of his emotions,
not knowing if she walked or crawled. Only the
growing force of Lee's feelings confirmed that she
was moving in the right direction. It seemed an
eternity before her wildly flailing hand hit and
clung to something solid. A kind of electricity
flowed through her fingers at the contact. She
pulled close and clung desperately.

Like a swiftly turning tide the chaos envelop-
ing her senses began to recede. She heard Lee's
voice dimly calling as though from a distant mountain peak. She shouted in answer. The earth stabilized under her and she realized that she was
indeed standing on her two feet, though leaning at
a precarious angle.

"Don't move," he shouted, his words
strengthening moment by moment. "Wait until I
strike a light."

With a click the pale flame of his lighter broke the mirror surface of the dark and the last of the chattering eddies swirled away into nothingness.

Eliza gasped and pulled Lee toward her, hurting her arm in her haste. He stumbled and held her tight. They stood in an alcove off the main passage beside a rotting wooden platform. The lighter flame revealed long rents in its decayed boards, and beneath them a fathomless blackness. The platform was barely sound enough to support its own weight, let alone the weight of a human being.

"It must be the old well under the east wing that Hale used to fill the cistern," Lee said, his voice thin. "I was following the sound of your voice through the darkness. I almost walked over it."

"The bones," Eliza said. "Where are they?"

Lee glanced at the well. The gaps in the boards were not wide enough to accommodate a skull. He left the alcove and began to search anxiously back along the brick walkway by the flame of the lighter. Eliza followed with a sinking feeling in her heart.

"It's all right," he said.

The glow of an oil lamp brightened the stone walls, and she saw the sack of bones lying in a heap where he had placed it while rummaging in his pockets for his lighter. Her own lamp lay shattered next to the black hulk of the furnace.

"We have a weapon," he said grimly, scooping up the sack. "It knows, and it doesn't like it. Let's get out of here."

# 17

"Allan, I don't want to hear any more about it," Hale said. "What you've proposed is madness."

"It will work," Allan said, spacing his words evenly. "Tell him, Lee."

"I think Allan's idea has a chance," Lee said.

"A chance," Hale repeated with a scowl. "And if it fails, we will have provoked the entity just as it is reaching its greatest destructive potential."

"If we don't act we're finished," Allan said.

"We don't know that," said Hale. "I won't be responsible for any more deaths."

The argument over how to use the remains of Michael Brannon, and whether they should be used at all, had smoldered all the previous evening, only to flare up after breakfast. Hale was set against any action whatever. Allan seemed equally determined not to passively await his fate. This placed Lee in the unenviable position of mediator.

The bones lay stretched across the conference table where Hale had arranged them the night

before in the shape of a human skeleton. They were
pathetically small, filling less than half the tabletop.
Michael Brannon had been a slight child, Eliza
thought as she gazed over them. Not at all like his
father. The boy must have followed his mother's
side of the family. The bones of the shins curved
slightly, leading Hale to speculate that the boy had
suffered from rickets in addition to his madness.

If he was ever mad at all. Perhaps he had been
autistic, or learning-impaired, or epileptic. In the
Victorian age all abnormals were lumped together.
What was madness but a vague term for the
unknown? She would be called mad for feeling the
emotions of other people. If she had been unstable
as a child, or less secretive about her ability, today
she might be locked in an institution, like her
mother. Sometimes she wondered if her mother's
insanity stemmed from an effort to suppress an
inherited empathic ability. Maybe all empaths were
destined to go mad, sooner or later.

"My decision is final," Hale said in a louder
voice that drew Eliza out of her reverie.

"I'm sorry, Professor," said Allan gravely. "I
can no longer accept your authority. You're allowing your sense of guilt to overpower your rational
judgement."

"I don't need any pop psychology from you,
young man." Hale wagged his blunt finger at
Allan. "With your history of drug abuse, you're
lucky I even let you into this seminar."

"We all feel so lucky," Amber said in a cutting tone.

Allan motioned her to be silent.

"I intend to compose the ritual with or without your help," he told Hale.

He was completely calm—almost detached from the conversation. It was as though he were describing the inevitable rather than presenting an argument. Hale, by contrast, threatened to explode from internal pressure. His flushed face gleamed with sweat.

"You're talking about necromancy—the same kind of bloody black magic that called the Messenger into being in the first place."

Allan shrugged.

"Sometimes one has to fight fire with fire."

Hale turned to Lee in exasperation.

"Lee, you talk to him. Make him see sense. I can't seem to get through his drug-induced stupor."

Lee shook his head.

"I agree that what Allan proposes is dangerous, but we have to act. If there were any other way—"

"There is," Hale said. "We take our supplies into the black room and seal the door, then simply wait out the New Year."

"There's no guarantee we'd be safe in the black room," Lee said. "The Messenger could easily smoke us out if it couldn't reach us directly."

"Even if we could escape by running and hiding, we can't simply let this entity continue to exist," Allan said with determination. "We have a responsibility to end it. That's why you came here."

This appeal to his sense of duty stifled the retort on Hale's lips. His broad shoulders sagged.

He turned his back on Allan and went to the table, where he stood looking down at the skeleton of the child.

Eliza expected Amber to protest this altruism, but she merely linked her arm through Allan's and stayed by him.

"Many crimes have been committed," Lee said, coming up behind Hale. "But the worst was against that boy. His soul has been in torment for nearly a century due to the monstrous evil of the one person in the world he should have been able to trust."

"For Mary's sake," Amber said quietly.

Hale turned to them, his face set in stubborn lines.

"I have no power over you if you refuse to accept my authority."

"That's not enough," said Allan. "We all have to work together if we're to have any chance of winning."

"Well, if you're all against me—" Hale looked at each of them. "And I see that you are—naturally I won't obstruct you."

Allan went over to Hale. He stood looking at the older man eye to eye.

"I'm asking for your help," he said simply.

Hale blinked and cleared his throat. He looked away, embarrassed by Allan's directness.

"I'll do all I can."

"Thank you, sir." Allan opened a spiral notebook on a bare corner of the table next to the bones. "I've made some sketches of the layout of the circle. I'd like your opinion."

Hale followed him and leaned over to look at the notebook. Hesitantly he put his hand on Allan's shoulder. It was perhaps as close as he could come to an apology.

Amber went to the opposite side of Allan and put her arm around his waist while he explained his ideas.

"We've postulated that the power of the Messenger is increasing exponentially, and will reach its peak at midnight on New Year's Eve, which is tomorrow. For this plan to work it must be put into effect on the anniversary of the Messenger's birth, but during the day when the spirit of Michael Brannon is strongest. We don't dare delay until tomorrow night ..."

"I'd like to catch my breath," Eliza said softly to Lee. Do you mind walking with me?"

He studied her with concern. She realized that her face must betray more of her inner turmoil than she wished.

Without waiting for his answer she left the gathering room and went quickly into the front hall toward the stairs. She needed light and chill fresh air. Lee followed her. As she mounted the staircase she slowed her pace to allow him to catch up.

"I can't stand arguments," she said. "Especially between friends."

"You should have left sooner."

"I didn't want to draw attention to myself."

He trailed her silently into the east wing. Her steps led automatically to her room. The door stood open. She went in. Because of its size the four-

poster had not been stripped of its mattress. A dis-
carded red blanket and a single pillow lay rumpled
across it.

Eliza walked past the naked frame of Amber's
bed to the window and looked down. It was a
sunny day. The snow lay deep from the last storm.
Automatically she searched for the lurking figure of
Mohan. They had not heard him outside the gathering room for several hours. He was nowhere to be
seen, but his footprints were visible in the snow.

A faint musky odor hung in the frigid air of
the room. It was elusive yet familiar. She turned,
trying to trace it. Lee stood in the doorway as
though afraid his nearness would be unwelcome.
She walked around the room slowly. The scent was
gone, leaving her wondering if she had imagined it.

Her eyes strayed to the bed. Two depressions
dimpled the pillow. In the middle of the twisted
blanket was a small white stain. She sat on the bed
and laid her hand in a hollow of the pillow, then
cradled her face. Quietly she began to cry.

"What's wrong?" Lee said, stepping into the
room. He gently pulled her hand away.

"Nothing. I'm an ass," she said, wiping her
eyes.

She was furious at her display of weakness.

"Tell me."

She gestured behind her at the bed.

"Amber and Allan. When they came up here
yesterday they made love."

He looked at the bed with a bemused expression.

"Even if they did, I don't see what there is to cry about."

"That's why she was acting like a blushing bride," Eliza said. "She didn't contradict him all morning."

He sat on the bed beside her.

"Why don't you tell me what's really bothering you?"

Eliza sighed and wiped her hand on the knee of her jeans.

"I don't know—maybe I'm jealous."

"Of Allan?" he said in surprise.

"No, Amber. She has something I can never have."

"Why can't you?" He covered her hand with his on her knee. "All you have to do is ask."

"It's not the sex, it's afterwards that hurts."

"Everyone takes a chance."

"It's harder for me."

"You have to stop worrying about tomorrow. Everyone feels hurt when their trust is betrayed. You just feel it more."

"I can't live with it."

"You have to."

"I'm afraid it will turn me into a stone-faced heartless old maid."

He laughed.

"What's so funny?" she asked defensively.

"I was trying to picture you in a rocking chair with granny glasses."

She slapped him spitefully on the side of the head. He caught her hand and embraced her with care so as not to injure her other arm, kissing her despite her resistance. Suddenly she knew she wanted him.

He shut the door. They undressed without haste and made love slowly side by side on the bed with their legs entwined. She was amazed by his control. Several times she reached shattering peaks of sensation before his own release. When it came, the strength of his reaction frightened her. He was like a whirling fire-wheel throwing off sparks to her empathic perception. She felt the intensity of his pleasure more forcefully than she had felt her own.

Afterwards they lay together with the blanket pulled over them against the freezing air. Eliza rubbed her bare shoulder. It felt pebbly. She realized her entire body was covered with goose bumps. Lee put his arm under her head and hugged her close for warmth.

"You should have told me," she said.

"Told you what?"

"That Hermetists make such terrific lovers. I might have given in sooner."

"You're not so bad yourself."

"Hollow flattery."

"Not at all. You seem to know just what to do at exactly the right moment. Maybe it's your gift."

"Anyway, we're a heck of a couple."

"You said it. It would be a shame to split up such a pair as us."

His flippant remark subdued her.

"We will have to go separate ways," she said. "I know it sounds corny, but we really are two ships passing in the night."

"You're right—it does sound corny."

"Be serious, Lee. I don't want to lose you."

"I don't want to lose you, either. Where's the problem?"

"Life is the problem," she said in exasperation. "You have your work in upper state New York. I have school in Toronto. We live unconnected lives. Our meeting is a freak. It isn't part of anything that belongs to either of us."

"You know your problem?" he said in a tone only half serious. "You think negatively. You're always preoccupied with what you can't do, instead of doing what you can."

"What have you ever done that you can preach about?" she retorted. "I bet life was always easy for you."

"Would you believe I was once an overweight, pimple-faced kid with asthma?"

She looked at him.

"Not hardly."

"It's true, though. One day I had an asthma attack that nearly killed me. I was away from home. No one knew what to do. I decided afterwards that the world wasn't about to change to accommodate me, so I'd better change myself until I could handle the world."

"Through magic?"

He nodded.

"What did your parents say about that?"

Lee breathed a deep sigh.

"My father was a Baptist minister. I was supposed to follow in his footsteps. You might say I was cut out for the cloth."

"You, a minister?" Eliza laughed.

"That's what I said."

"What happened?"

"We had a parting of the ways."

"I hope he's not still mad at you."

"He's dead," Lee said quietly.

"Lee, I'm sorry."

"Don't be." He smiled at her. "We made it up before the end. He wasn't such a bad old coot—just too much starch in his collar."

A flicker of movement caught her eye. She looked past the foot of the bed toward the small chest of drawers, which had been shoved at an angle into the corner. A grotesque parody of a human face leered at her from the oval mirror. She screamed and clutched at Lee.

It was an instant before she realized the face was only a reflected image. She turned to the window in time to see Mohan thrust his bare hand through one of the panes of glass. Jagged shards flew inward with a crash that echoed through the house. He began to tear at the wooden cross-frame without regard to the remaining sharp spears of glass lacerating his palm. His face twisted and writhed in a snarling, frost-bitten mask of horror.

In a single motion Lee rolled out of the bed and picked up one of the unlit kerosene heaters from the floor. He ran toward the window and threw the heater at the glass with all the force of his upper body. The window exploded outward. The heater struck Mohan in the face. He grunted and flailed his arms as he fell slowly backward. Lee had to catch himself against the sill of the window to keep from following the heater to the snowy ground below.

Eliza hurried toward him.

"Watch your feet," he said sharply.

She stopped, realizing that the floorboards were covered with broken transparent splinters. His own feet left red oozing marks as he went to the bed and gathered up the blanket, then threw it over the glass fragments.

"Lee, you're bleeding—"

He leaned out through the hole in the window and looked down. She came up behind him.

"Is he dead?"

"Take a look."

There was no body in the drift of snow that lay close to the house, only a broken section of gray pipe and the fractured heater.

"He climbed up the lead drainpipe," Lee said. "It tore loose when he grabbed for it."

Footsteps pounded in the corridor. The door burst open and the others rushed in, then stopped to stare. Eliza realized she was naked. She dived for her pile of clothes and held them before her. Blushing, she struggled to dress without exposing herself.

Lee seemed completely unconscious of his nudity. He made no attempt to cover himself as he calmly explained what had happened.

Hale gave a silent but emphatic curse.

"I should have guessed he could climb the pipes. It's a wonder he didn't do it sooner."

"Don't blame yourself," Allan said. "No ordinary man could make that climb."

"We'd better lock all the upstairs rooms from the outside," Lee said. "If he gets in another window, the door may slow him down.

"Lee, your feet," Amber said in alarm. "You're bleeding."

"Come downstairs and we'll treat those cuts. Then we'll tell you what we've been cooking up for tomorrow." Hale glanced wryly at Lee's nakedness. "Better put on some clothes. You're liable to catch a chill."

Lee began to dress. Eliza caught Amber looking at her with a cat-like smile of amusement. At another time it might have irritated her. But she realized there was no hostility in the look, only playfulness. Eliza felt alert and intensely alive. She suddenly saw the amusing aspect of her position and could not help laughing out loud.

Lee stopped midway into his briefs and turned to look at her past his naked buttocks.

"It's not that funny," he said dryly.

# 18

"Hurry," Hale said. "It's nearly sunset."

They pressed around each other in the windowless storage room just outside the door to the black chamber. Preparations for the ritual had consumed more time than anticipated. As the shadows of afternoon lengthened, Haven had gradually taken on an atmosphere of electric tension.

It was New Year's Eve, the very day Brannon had worked his remorseless will on the powers of darkness nearly a century ago. In this room mad children—who knew how many?—had died horrible, painful deaths to satisfy his warped illusion of destiny. There was a sense of gathering malice all about them that waited only the fall of night to unleash its hellish potency.

Eliza was the first to enter. She stopped on the threshold and drew in her breath. An imposing draped figure, its cowled face in shadow, confronted her with its arms crossed on its breast. For a moment she thought Daniel P. Brannon had

returned from the grave. Then the figure threw back
the hood and stepped aside to let her pass, and she
recognized the strained pale profile of Allan.

He was dressed in the magical regalia from
Brannon's trunk. The circlet of silver bound a
square of folded cloth into a cap on his head. On
the breast of the midnight blue robe hung the massive silver and gold lamen. A multicolored sash
closed the robe. The ebony rod was thrust into it.
On his feet he wore painted leather sandals.

Silently he indicated one of the points of a
large chalk pentagram drawn in white on the black
floorboards. She blinked water from her eyes as she
took her position upon it. The air hung thick with
acrid incense smoke that fumed from a charcoal
brazier inside a red chalk triangle. A burning lamp
in each corner of the room etched the serpentine
plumes that arose from its glowing iron bowl
against the blackness.

The triangle measured about three feet on
each side, its base fronting a point of the pentagram. Inside it before the brazier rested the skull of
Michael Brannon. The sightless eye sockets seemed
to stare up at Eliza with mute accusation. The two
thigh bones of the child lay crossed in front of the
skull, reminding her of a pirate flag.

In the open space in the middle of the pentagram were arrayed a curved knife with a black hilt,
a small silver chalice, and a flat earthenware dish
with a granular white substance heaped upon it.

Allan pointed to where each of the others
should stand as they successively entered the

chamber. Eliza realized that she was on the left leg of the pentagram. Lee took his position on the right leg. Amber stood opposite her on the right arm. Hale stopped on the left arm of the star to Eliza's left. Allan closed the chamber door and sealed it with an occult gesture, then stepped onto the head of the pentagram and faced them with his back to the red triangle.

"Before we start I want everyone to clearly understand the danger of this experiment," Hale said. "Now is the time to withdraw."

"Quiet, please," said Allan in a toneless voice.

He bowed his head to meditate.

The harsh emotions of the previous day had not completely subsided. Even though Hale lent his support to the ritual he remained far from enthusiastic. Eliza could feel the nervous darting of his worried thoughts, and knew he was not fearful for himself, but held himself responsible for their welfare. He was afraid of any action that might put a life in jeopardy.

Allan raised his head.

"We are gathered here to summon forth the tortured spirit of Michael Brannon and give it rest. Remain unafraid, for our purpose is justified."

He lifted his arms and looked heavenward, speaking a short prayer in a strange guttural language. Eliza wondered if it was the Enochian from which letters were inscribed on the back of the lamen. It sounded like a cross between Greek and Arabic to her untutored ears.

Allan went to the center of the pentagram and took up the clay dish in his cupped hands. Returning to his place, he reverently touched his tongue to the white powder that lay on it. He passed it to Amber on his left.

"Taste of your mortality," he said.

Amber imitated his gesture, tipping her tongue against the substance on the dish, and passed it to Lee, who did the same and passed it to Eliza. Hesitantly Eliza raised the dish and put out her tongue. The familiar flavor reassured her. It was salt, nothing more. She passed the dish to Hale. He tasted the salt and gave it back into the hands of Allan.

"Our flesh comes of earth. To earth it returns."

There was a dolorous note in his voice that chilled them all. Allan replaced the dish and turned to face the skull and bones in the triangle. He drew out the black rod and raised it overhead. Although Eliza could not see clearly because his back was toward her, he seemed to grip the lamen hanging about his neck in his left hand.

"Hear me, Michael Brannon! I summon you by the power of these consecrated symbols which you know well. Return to your former house of clay. Manifest forth in the triangle appointed to you, for it is the will of your Father in heaven that you be given peace."

The smoke-filled air above the brazier in the triangle shimmered and swirled, but nothing further happened. Allan turned calmly and slid the rod back under his sash, and Eliza realized he had only given the preliminary evocation. He had not expected the spirit to respond.

"Revolve the pentagram," he said.

Eliza began to walk along the chalk line toward Allan, who at the same time started toward Lee. All of them followed the line of chalk that formed the left side of the point of the star upon which they stood.

When she reached Allan's point she stopped and faced the center of the pentagram.

"Zacare, ca, od zamran," they all chanted in unison.

Allan had made them memorize the series of Enochian words the previous evening. It was a potent evocation commanding the spirit to coalesce and reveal itself.

Eliza walked toward the point where formerly Lee had stood, but which was now occupied by Allan. The pentagram revolved another fifth turn. Again they recited the words, this time in more confident voices. They continued on around the chalk lines in a clockwise direction, pausing at each point to chant, until once again they found themselves in their original places.

As the pentagram revolved a subtle change took place in the air of the chamber. It was not so much a physical as a psychic transformation. When Eliza shut her eyes the darkness behind her lids pulsed and flickered with colored bursts like fireworks. She became dizzy and felt as though she were standing in the dark on a high place. When she opened her eyes these impressions retreated but did not entirely depart.

"Kneel," Allan ordered.

Following his example, they knelt on the arms of the pentagram facing inward. Amber's full lips were compressed and her jaw tight. Lee gave the impression of controlled excitement. Eliza glanced at Hale. His brow gleamed with sweat even though the room was cool.

Allan reached forward and drew toward him the black-hilted knife and the silver chalice. With a single quick motion he cut himself with the knife across the left palm, then allowed his blood to drip into the cup. When the drops ceased to fall he pushed the chalice toward Amber and handed her the knife.

She took it with surprise and cast a questioning look at Allan. This part of the ritual had not been mentioned.

"It's necessary," he murmured.

Still she hesitated, looking at each of them. Lee nodded to her slightly. Hale gave no sign. Biting her lip, she pressed the point of the knife into the heel of her left hand. The steel indented her milk-white skin. She closed her eyes and flicked the point across her palm.

Eliza flinched, feeling the pain of the other woman as her own. The blood seemed to pause before it welled into the line of the cut and trickled freely into the chalice. In her apprehension Amber had cut deeper than she had intended. It was a minute before the scarlet droplets slowed. She put the cut to her lips and with her other hand slid the knife and cup to Lee, who opened his palm emotionlessly before passing the knife to Eliza.

Her hand trembled as she took it. The sight of blood on the polished steel made her squeamish. She felt a faintness and firmly beat it down inside herself. This was no time to be weak. Gritting her resolution, she detached herself from her fear and made a small cut on her left palm where it extended from under the bandage, then held the cup close beneath her sling as six or seven drops fell into it. Quickly she passed the chalice to Hale, who bled himself with a single efficient stroke.

Allan gathered in the chalice with both hands and tipped it to his lips, then gave it to Amber.

"Taste of your immortality."

With a grimace Amber tasted the blood and passed the cup to Lee. It quickly rounded the pentagram. Eliza was startled by the rush of animal strength that suffused her limbs at its salty, metallic flavor. In giving up a portion of her own vitality, she realized, she had partaken of the life forces of four others. The level of energy in the chamber quadrupled, and the air began to vibrate with a low hum that could be felt rather than heard.

Allan got up from his knees and indicated for them to also rise. Turning, he emptied the remainder of the blood over the triangle. He poured half on the glowing embers in the brazier and half on the skull. Steam went up where the warm blood touched the cold bone. The smell of the incense grew more earthy. He replaced the chalice in the

center of the pentagram, then faced the skull and
spoke to it in a resonant voice.

"Michael Brannon! Your hunger compels you
to reveal yourself. I command you, come forth!"

With the black rod he traced an emblem on
the smokey air over the triangle and vibrated a
series of barbarous words that were even harsher
than the previous Enochian phrase. The cut in
Eliza's palm throbbed by some hidden sympathy.
Allan mutely pointed the rod at the skull. There fell
a sudden calm broken only by the tense breaths of
the watchers. Even the writhing column of incense
seemed frozen in space.

A distant boom echoed through the floor
beneath their feet. None of them dared move. The
silence continued for the space of over a minute.
When the tension was becoming unbearable Eliza
heard a shuffling step outside the door of the black
chamber. She listened while the steps dragged
across the floor of the storage room. An image of
Mary's frozen corpse rose in her mind. She stared
wide-eyed at Lee. He gave her a look of reassur-
ance and she felt the strength of his courage. She
turned with him to watch the door. The footsteps
halted just outside it.

Without warning the door exploded into a
million fragments. Eliza shielded her face from the
flying splinters and nearly fell. Lee caught her
elbow and held her steady. As the dust and billow-
ing incense smoke parted she saw a shadow
framed in the naked doorway. It stood swaying just
outside the plane of the room.

"Mohan!" Amber exclaimed.

Allan raised his hand for silence.

The brown face of the Sikh twisted with fury and his eyes rolled. He was scarcely recognizable beneath the mask of his swollen features. Patches of gray on his nose and cheeks indicated severe frost-bite. Eliza cringed when she looked at his hands. They were mere broken slabs of exposed bone and bloody flesh.

A dark mass crawled over his shoulders like a thick cloak of shadow. It played about his face, from time to time obscuring it completely. At these moments his features transformed into those of a snarling beast and his eyes became burning points of fire. Then the ugliness would melt and reveal the ravaged human visage beneath.

"Enter, Michael," Allan said. "The circle is open to you."

The thing surged forward, its face suffused with killing lust. It stopped and swayed, baffled by the magical barrier of protection around the room, which Allan had renewed. Although the door was gone, the barrier remained intact. Through the shifting smoke Eliza saw the thin silver ribbon of the occult circle spanning the gap at heart level with a pale unearthly glow.

"By this rod and lamen of your father, come forth and show yourself!"

It writhed in impotent fury, its limbs rippling as light and shade played across them. Raising its arms, it pressed inward. The barrier supported its weight. Eliza watched with horror its broken fingers claw and dig at the strangely solid air.

"Zacare, ca, od zamran!" Allan chanted rhythmically.

Some instinct made Eliza chant with him, and the rest followed her example. She felt herself lifted and borne up on the words, an organ in a vast living body of immense power. The chalk lines of the pentagram transformed into channels of vital force that linked her spiritually to its power points. She became five-fold. Lee and the others were different aspects of herself, beautiful colors reflected in the facets of a single great jewel. Fear left her. She felt a deep welling forth of tranquil assurance.

"Zacare, ca, od zamran!"

Each chanted word of the evocation buffeted the air and made the lamps at the corners of the room flicker. The thing that wore Mohan's shell cringed away and tried to withdraw, only to find itself caught like an unwitting fish on the endless string of words. Eliza observed it passionlessly from the height of her altered perspective as it twisted and fought desperately for release. The awful power of their five-fold will could not be broken. Inexorably they began to reel in the human half of the Messenger, tearing the unholy entity apart.

"Zacare, ca, od zamran!"

It threw back its head and howled. Even from her stellar altitude the agony in the sound touched Eliza, who knew that it did not issue solely from a human throat. The thing began to thrash and beat at Mohan's face with his mangled hands, reacting with the self-destructive impulse of a wild beast caught in a trap. An unseen force gripped his body and shook it violently. One of his flailing fingers struck him in the eye. The vacantly staring orb dissolved into a pulp of bloody fluid. Eliza tried to turn her head, but the power that held the thing held her also and she could not look away.

The howling cut off as with the stroke of a knife and the body of Mohan collapsed into a pathetic heap of disjointed limbs. At the same instant Allan broke off the chant. Eliza observed without surprise that she and the others also stopped on the same syllable.

In the smoke above the red triangle a pale standing form slowly began to coalesce within a shimmering cloud. The upper half of the apparition solidified into the head and naked torso of a young boy. His face shone with an angelic light. Brown curling hair hung over his high forehead almost to the level of his blue eyes. His nose was snub and his parted lips feminine.

He trembled and stared about with a vague and fearful wonder. When he saw the robed figure facing him a contented smile of recognition soothed his features. He reached out his arms but did not seem able to touch Allan, although they stood quite close.

"I'm tired," the boy said in a high wavering voice. "Can I go back to bed now, father?"

Allan raised the black rod in both hands, the gold caps hidden in each fist, and extended it horizontally over the head of the boy.

"Sleep, Michael," he said.

Eliza started and stared hard at his back. It was not Allan's voice but the deeper, more powerful voice of an older man.

A look of pure joy overspread the face of the apparition. Like a distant object obscured by mist, it faded moment by moment until it was gone.

Allan did not turn or speak. The others stood silent for several seconds. Eliza felt the force that bound them together into one spiritual organism slipping away. Hale let out a heavy breath.

"It's over," he said wearily. "Thank God."

"Wait," Lee said. He pointed to the doorway. "Something's happening."

Wisps of smoke rose from the curved back of Mohan's crumpled body. While they watched in shock more began to stream from its limbs. The smoke thickened and spread as it roiled upward. With a sudden burst of heat and light the hair of the corpse caught fire and blazed. Eliza put her hand over her mouth and coughed as oily, noxious fumes from the burning flesh enveloped her.

With horrible rapidity the body shriveled inward upon itself. White bones became visible among the flames. In moments even these crumbled to ashes. Where the corpse had lain remained only a charred and blackened depression in the floor.

Framed in the open doorway reared a bright and awful presence. Fire crowned its head and sparks danced in its eyes. It shimmered in a shifting radiant cloak that might have been a garment or a part of its form, and seemed to float like a flame on the air. Eliza felt a wild ecstasy emanating from it that was not emotion as she knew it but more a definition of its being. The face it turned upon them was of unearthly and terrible beauty.

# 19

As the shimmering image hovered in the doorway the paint on the jamb curled and burst into flames. Eliza felt the awesome power of its heat even at a distance of several paces. It beat against her face and hands like the summer sun.

"The Salamander," Lee shouted over the roar of the flames. "There's nothing left to bind it."

As though understanding his words, the elemental raised its slender arms above its head. Tongues of fire radiated from them like the pinions of a phoenix. With an expression of celestial disdain it turned its back on the watching humans and drifted away across the storage room, growing brighter with each moment. Where it passed, the walls exploded and began to burn with furious intensity.

Eliza felt Lee's arms about her. She hugged him and stumbled as he led her toward the flaming rectangle of the doorway. The intense heat drove them back, but not before Eliza saw that the entire storage room and the corridor beyond it were one great mass of burning. This time it was no illusion. The smoke choked and seared her lungs. She began to cough and could not stop. Lee was shouting something at her but she could not hear him above the roar.

There's no other way out, she thought. Lee, Lee, I'm sorry we didn't have more time.

A robed figure crossed in front of her blurred sight. She blinked and wiped her streaming eyes with her palm. What she saw could not be. Yet the image remained distinct through the rippling air.

In the antique magical costume Allan had been wearing stood the tall and powerfully built Daniel P. Brannon. He stared at her with piercing dark eyes as though with recognition. Moving with an aura of authority to the blazing doorway, he turned his back on the flames and spread his arms so that his body formed a great cross. The voluminous sleeves of his robe blocked out the scorching heat.

Amber stumbled against Eliza. She supported the hunched and coughing Hale with her shoulder. Eliza took hold of Hale under his other arm. Lee put his hand on her shoulder. Eliza could barely recognize him through the smoke. She glanced around but did not see Allan.

The robed figure turned toward the fire and stepped into the flames. Remarkably he did not burn. He looked over his shoulder and made a motion for the others to follow.

"Come on," Lee shouted, his lips close to her ear. She barely heard him.

He marshaled them after the ghostly Brannon, who turned his back on them with finality and walked into the solid yellow wall of fire. Eliza went first after him. She felt Hale's hands pressed against her shoulders, but not the flames that licked and fanned over her body. All around her was uniform blazing light. She could not see where she was or where she was going, but desperately pursued the dark blue robe that danced before her vision.

A crash startled her and made her look behind. Only then did she realize that she was standing outside the house in the snow on the front lawn. Haven was one mass of flames from end to end. She could not remember leaving the house. Another wrenching crash sounded as part of the roof fell in. Suddenly exhausted, Eliza sat down in the snow and watched the windows explode outward one by one with the force of shotgun blasts.

Somehow she and the others had managed to reach the middle of the lawn, a safe distance from the consuming fire. A solid pillar of black smoke mounted the still twilight air into a leaden sky. There were periodic crackles as timbers fell in, and a great explosion of sparks as one of the chimneys toppled slowly backward.

Her mind began to function once more. She looked around for Lee and saw him crouched over the robed Allan, who lay motionless on the snow with his arms spread. Amber and Hale stood nearby gazing down with concern. Their clothes were scorched and soot-stained, but their faces and hands were unburned. Eliza went over and knelt beside Lee. For the first time she noticed the coldness of the snow against her knees through her corduroy pants.

"Is he hurt?"

Lee gave her a worried look.

"I can't tell. He won't wake up."

"What happened?"

"You saw—when he got out he just collapsed."

"I must have blacked out."

"Are you all right?" He studied her face.

"I guess so. What happened to Brannon?"

Lee stared at her.

"I meant Brannon's ghost," she said, looking at Amber and Hale.

They did not answer but watched her nervously.

"You must have seen him," she said with a frown. "He led us through the fire."

"Allan led us out," Hale said. "God knows how, but he did it."

"No, it was Brannon," she said forcefully.

"What did you see?"

Eliza related her version of the escape from the house.

"You must have been hallucinating," Hale told her. "We were all nearly overcome by the smoke."

Allan coughed and sat up. He groaned and put his head in his hands, drawing up his knees to rest his elbows on.

"What the devil happened?" he said. "How did we get out in the snow?"

"Don't you remember?" Lee said.

"Sorry." Allan looked up with a rueful smile. "After I spoke the final evocation I blacked out."

Lee related what had taken place, and repeated Eliza's remarks about Brannon.

"So that's what possession feels like."

Allan got up slowly and beat the snow off the hem of his robe.

"You think that's what happened?" Hale asked.

"Had to be. I'd like to play hero, but I didn't lead anyone anywhere. I don't even remember banishing the boy's spirit."

With a low rumble another of the stone chimneys toppled down and took part of a wall with it. A curtain of sparks rose against the black smoke like stars. The towering flames were bright orange in the gathering gloom.

"There goes everything," Hale said softly. "My notes. My video tapes. My research material. Brannon's diary."

"More to the point," said Amber, "There goes our clothes, our blankets, our food, and our heaters."

"Someone may see the flames," Allan said.

"Not thirty miles away," said Lee. "We better prepare ourselves to wait out the full stay."

"Lee's right," said Hale. "I'm going to see if I can break the lock on the stable. At least it will give us shelter."

"I thought you had the key," Amber said.

"I left it in the house. It's probably a pool of molten brass by now. Coming Allan? I may need you to go in through the window."

"Why not?" Allan said cheerfully.

He plodded through the snow after Hale, looking both impressive and ridiculous in his long blue robe. At the top of the lawn he turned and motioned back to Amber.

"Come and watch."

Amber glanced at Lee, then at Eliza. She shrugged.

"Why not."

They stood together following Amber with their eyes as she trailed after the two men. She stayed well to the side of the burning house, which began to fall in upon itself in its final death throes.

Eliza turned to Lee and put her arm around his waist, pressing her cheek into his shoulder.

"I can't believe it's finally over."

"Believe it," he said, hugging her close. "Without Michael's confused spirit to bind it to Haven, the Salamander had no reason to stay. It returned to the elemental sphere where it belongs."

Eliza burrowed her face into his sweater, smelling his male scent under the smoke that still clung to it.

"I don't care if we are cold. At least cold is natural. We know how to fight it."

He stroked her hair tenderly.

"There's another kind of cold that's harder to fight."

She smiled.

"I think the fire thawed it out for good. I can't feel it anymore."

They kissed.

"What on earth are we going to tell the Mounties?" she murmured, her lips close to his ear.

"We tell them the truth," Lee said. "That Mohan went crazy, killed Mary, and burned down the house. We just don't go into detail."

"Do you think they'll buy it?"

"They won't have any alternative. The fire destroyed all the evidence."

She turned her gaze to the crumbling skeleton of the house.

"When you get back to school I'll come to see you," he promised.

"You'll be so far away—in another country."

"Just across the border. I'll drive up on weekends."

"Maybe I'll enroll in the Phoenix Institute next term."

"We'd be glad to get you," he said seriously. "We haven't got an empath."

"I'm a rare bird."

"You are indeed."

They were still kissing when they heard the bell. It rang crystal clear across the placid waters of the inlet. A lobster boat, its traps stacked high on its stern deck, came into view around the stony point. They waved and shouted. From the side of the boat a tiny figure waved back. His greeting carried faintly across the water.

# About the Magic

That a being of spirit and a creature of flesh might be fused to produce an unholy amalgam was a belief common throughout the ancient world. Usually the fusion was achieved by an act of sexual union. The result was of two kinds: either a spirit with earthy human qualities, or a human with the supernatural faculties of a spirit.

The early Jews believed that the Sumerian demoness Lilitu, whom they called Lilith, comes to men sleeping alone to steal their seed for the purpose of engendering spirits of the earthly realm—that is, spirits who are barred from ascending higher than the sphere of the Moon because of the weight of their material part. Substantially the same belief is found in the annals of the European witch trials, where Lilith has been replaced by the anonymous class of succubi, lustful female spirits who were considered to be either the Devil in disguise, or servants of Satan that steal semen from men who lie sleeping (see *The Malleus Maleficarum*,

Part I, Question 3). The result of these unions between spirit mothers and mortal fathers results in offspring of the first type.

In the Bible and at greater length in the Book of Enoch we find reference to the other type of amalgam, the progeny of human mothers and spirit fathers. The Bible refers to these unnatural offspring as "mighty men which were of old, men of renown" (Genesis 6:4). Again, during the witch trials the part of the lustful fallen angels was played by a class of spirits called incubi, male spirits having carnal knowledge of mortal women.

Although less common, a similar union of spirit and flesh might be brought about by magical means. Babies stolen by the fairies in European legend were said to be replaced by simulacra in every outward respect identical, save that these "changelings" were, like chicks hatched from the eggs of cuckoos, apt to grow faster and larger, cry more, and to be fay and strange. They were gifted with magical powers such as second sight. The great magician Merlin was reputed to be half-human and half-fairy.

In ancient times these mixed beings were by no means all evil. In fact they were noted for their wisdom and war skill. Many of the demigods of classical Greece such as Dionysus, Heracles and Aesculapius were engendered by gods on mortal women. However in Christian times such half-breeds came to be regarded as tainted, foredoomed by their inherent nature to commit acts of evil and serve the purposes of Satan.

"Salamander" was the name applied to Fire elementals by the German physician and magician Paracelsus, who lived at the beginning of the 16th century. He divided the spirits of the sublunary world into four classes based on the four elements then thought to compose all of nature—Fire, Air, Water and Earth. Fire elementals (spirits arising from one of the elements) he called Salamanders. Air elementals were Sylphs. Water elementals received the name Undines. Earth elementals were called Gnomes. Each class of elementals exhibits characteristics in harmony with its element. Thus Fire elementals are very hot-tempered, intense, consuming, bright, active, energetic, being both beautiful and terrible to look upon.

The name itself comes from the salamander lizard, which perhaps due to its coldness to the touch was fabled to live and thrive in the midst of flames. The power of this lizard over fire was a common and ancient belief. The Roman naturalist Pliny the Elder, writing around the time of Christ, records in his *Natural History* (Book X, Chapter 86) that salamanders extinguish fire on contact the way ice does. When the Italian Renaissance artist Benvenuto Cellini was five, he writes in his Autobiography that he, his father and his sister witnessed a salamander dancing in the flames of their fireplace.

Spirits such as Salamanders are summoned and commanded in formal Western magic by means of a very specific set of instruments and symbols. The contents of Brannon's trunk are a fair description of the working tools of a Victorian goetic theurgist—a ritual magician who works through demons or fallen angels. They have not changed materially in a thousand years and are still employed today. Those interested in some of the older forms of instruments will find them described and pictured in that greatest of Western grimoires, *The Key Of Solomon the King (Clavicula Salomonis)*, Book II, Chapter VIII.

The noted English magician of the reign of Elizabeth the First, Doctor John Dee, used a similar set of instruments to initially contact the angels who dictated, through his seer the alchemist Edward Kelley, the letters and writings of the Enochian language. The letters that appear on the back of Brannon's silver lamen do exist. They, along with the other letters of the Enochian alphabet, were psychically perceived by Kelley on May 6, 1583, when they appeared in a light yellow color on the page in front of him, allowing him to trace their outlines exactly with a pen before they faded from his sight.

The name of the angelic language comes from the biblical patriarch Enoch, who was taken up to heaven while still alive (Genesis 5:24) and thus was supposed to have dwelt with the angels and learned their wisdom. Enochian played a significant part in the magic of the Hermetic Order of the Golden Dawn, a secret occult society of Victorian England that contained among its members the famous poet W. B. Yeats and the infamous wizard Aleister Crowley. It would seem highly probable that Brannon was affiliated with the Golden Dawn, perhaps through his Masonic links—the founders of the Golden Dawn were Freemasons.

Along with the Enochian alphabet and language, Dee and Kelley received a set of nineteen different Keys or Calls intended to be used in the evocation of various orders of the angelic hierarchy. These Keys are both potent and poetic. Most of them contain some variation on the Enochian phrase *Zacare, ca, od zamran* (Move, therefore, and show yourselves), and it is these words, or their variants, that constitute the actual Enochian command of evocation that compels the spirits to appear visibly before the magician. The Keys form an integral part of the system of Hermetic magic used in the Golden Dawn, in the goetic theurgy of Aleister Crowley, and in the Satanism of Anton LaVey.

The evocation of the soul of Michael Brannon within a triangle on the floor of the black chamber, using smoke from incense and burning blood to lend his ghostly shade perceptible substance, is strictly in accord with the dark practices of necromancy. The raising of the ghosts of dead souls is extremely ancient. Usually it is done to gain knowledge only the dead may be expected to possess. In the Odyssey of the Greek poet Homer, written perhaps in the 8th century BC, the hero Odysseus travels to the Land of the Dead where he raises the shade of the prophet Teiresias the Theban to consult about his future. Following the detailed instructions of his lover, the sorceress Circe (*Odyssey*, Book X, lines 517-40), Odysseus attracts the ghost of Teiresias with the fumes of warm blood newly spilled from the throats of sacrificed black sheep. The pale shivering dead are unable to resist the lure of vital blood, which, as it says in the Bible, "is the life of all flesh" (Leviticus 17:14).

In medieval magic evil or dangerous spirits are evoked, or called forth into tangible presence, within the bounds of a triangle. The description of this figure is explicitly provided in the medieval grimoire of the *Lemegeton* or *Lesser Key of Solomon the King:* "it is to be Made 2 foot off [away] from the Circle, and 3 foot over [i.e. overall—three feet on each side]. Note. this [triangle] is to be Placed upon that Cost [i.e. coast, or direction of the compass] the Spirit Belongeth; etc—Observe the [Moon] in working, etc" (British Museum Sloane ms. 2731).

The magic circle in which the magician and his assistants stand provides a barrier impassible to the demons summoned into being within the triangle, and made visible by means of the rising smoke of incense and blood. To be perceived such spirits must take on a body of smoke or mist. In the black room the pentagram drawn in chalk on the floor with a single unbroken reflecting line takes the place of a more conventional circle, but is no less potent a protection. The unusual step of placing the triangle within the larger circle of silver established by Brannon is taken in order to use its power to rend the Messenger asunder. Michael Brannon is compelled to enter the triangle, yet the Salamander cannot pass the silver barrier—hence they must separate.

It remains for me to say a few words about tumo and lung gom lest the reader imagine that these are fabulous inventions. Both existed and were used by the magicians and Buddhist monks of Tibet down to modern times. They are a form of hatha (physical) yoga designed to enable an individual to survive in the harsh winter climate of the Himalayas. Tumo speeds up the metabolism of the body so that it actually becomes warm to the touch. Monks learning the technique were accustomed to engage in contests with each other, in which they sat in the snow naked and allowed wet sheets to be wrapped around their shoulders. The monk who dried the most sheets with tumo was declared the winner. Lung gom is a leaping run that allows rapid progress to be made through deep snow. Those who travel with lung gom do so in a waking trance, and appear to observers to be almost weightless (see the excellent description in Alexandra David-Neel's *Magic and Mystery In Tibet*, Chapter VI).

**THE THREE BOOKS OF OCCULT PHILOSOPHY**
**Completely Annotated, with Modern Commentary—The Foundation Book of Western Occultism**
**by Henry Cornelius Agrippa**
**edited and annotated by Donald Tyson**

Agrippa's *Three Books of Occult Philosophy* is the single most important text in the history of Western occultism. Occultists have drawn upon it for five centuries, although they rarely give it credit. First published in Latin in 1531 and translated into English in 1651, it has never been reprinted in its entirety since. Photocopies are hard to find and very expensive. Now, for the first time in 500 years, *Three Books of Occult Philosophy* will be presented as Agrippa intended. There were many errors in the original translation, but occult author Donald Tyson has made the corrections and has clarified the more obscure material with copious notes.

This is a necessary reference tool not only for all magicians, but also for scholars of the Renaissance, Neoplatonism, the Western Kabbalah, the history of ideas and sciences and the occult tradition. It is as practical today as it was 500 years ago.

**0-87542-832-0, 1,080 pgs., 7 x 10, softcover    $29.95**

# RITUAL MAGIC
## What It Is & How To Do It
### by Donald Tyson

For thousands of years men and women have practiced it despite the severe repression of sovereigns and priests. Now, *Ritual Magic* takes you into the heart of that entrancing, astonishing and at times mystifying secret garden of *magic*.

What is this ancient power? Where does it come from? How does it work? Is it mere myth and delusion, or can it truly move mountains and make the dead speak. . . bring rains from a clear sky and calm the seas. . . turn the outcome of great battles and call down the Moon from Heaven? Which part of the claims made for magic are true in the most literal sense, and which are poetic exaggerations that must be interpreted symbolically? How can magic be used to improve *your* life?

This book answers these and many other questions in a clear and direct manner. Its purpose is to separate the wheat from the chaff and make sense of the non-sense. It explains what the occult revival is all about, reveals the foundations of practical ritual magic, showing how modern occultism grew from a single root into a number of clearly defined esoteric schools and pagan sects.

0-87542-835-5, 288 pgs., 6 x 9, illus., index, softcover                                    $12.95

**RUNE MAGIC**
**by Donald Tyson**

Drawing upon historical records, poetic fragments, and the informed study of scholars, *Rune Magic* resurrects the ancient techniques of this tactile form of magic and integrates those methods with modern occultism so that anyone can use the runes in a personal magical system. For the first time, every known and conjectured meaning of all 33 known runes, including the 24 runes known as "futhark", is available in one volume. In addition, *Rune Magic* covers the use of runes in divination, astral traveling, skrying, and on amulets and talismans. A complete rune ritual is also provided, and 24 rune worlds are outlined. Gods and Goddesses of the runes are discussed, with illustrations from the National Museum of Sweden.

**0-87542-826-6, 224 pgs., 6 x 9, softcover          $9.95**

## RUNE MAGIC CARDS
### by Donald Tyson

Llewellyn Publications presents, for the first time ever, Rune Magic Cards created by Donald Tyson. This unique divinatory deck consists of 24 strikingly designed cards, boldly portraying a Germanic "futhark" rune on each card. Robin Wood has illuminated each rune card with graphic illustrations done in the ancient Norse tradition. Included on each card are the old English name, its meaning, the phonetic value of the rune, and its number in Roman numerals. Included with this deck is a complete instruction booklet, giving the history and origins, ways of using the cards for divination, and magical workings, sample spreads and a wealth of information culled from years of study.
**0-87542-827-4, 24 two-color cards,**
**48-pg. booklet**                                          **$12.95**

## HOW TO MAKE AND USE A MAGIC MIRROR
**Psychic Windows into New Worlds**
**by Donald Tyson**

Tyson takes you step-by-step through the creation of this powerful mystical tool. You will learn about: tools and supplies needed to create the mirror; construction techniques; how to use the mirror for scrying (divination); how to communicate with spirits; and how to use the mirror for astral travel.

Tyson also presents a history of mirror lore in magic and literature. For anyone wanting their personal magical tool, *How to Make and Use a Magic Mirror* is a must item.

**0-87542-831-2, 176 pgs., mass market, illus.    $3.95**

**CASTLE OF DECEPTION**
**A Novel of Sorcery and Swords and Other-Worldly Matters**
**with Seven Short Essays on the Reality of Matters Supernatural**
**by Ed Fitch, illustrated by Bill Fugate**

Here are demons, and spell vs. counterspell, and the magick of sex in witch-rites so the Good may triumph over Evil!

Here is the lust of Vampire-Sorceress held bondage to Demon King, and used to enthrall the Blond Witch-Queen so that her magic to defeat the demon is thwarted.

Here is the Lord and Lady of Wolves who turn their own special magic to the aid of Tanithia the Witch and her Lover, and teach them to shape-change and flee to safety with the world pack.

Here is the Witch-finder, whose blind fanaticism places him in inadvertent service to the demons, and nearly prevents Tanithia's final victory over the dark forces.

The seven short essays at the end of the book include The Reality of Demons, Vampirism, Ritual Magick, Animal Communication, Shape-Changing, Sex Magick, and Witchcraft.
**0-87542-231-4, 304 pgs., 5 1/4 x 8, softcover     $6.95**

**THE COMMITTEE**
**by Raymond Buckland**

*"Duncan's eyes were glued to the destruct button. He saw that the colonel's hand never did get to it. Yet, even as he watched, he saw the red button move downwards, apparently of its own volition. The rocket blew into a million pieces, and the button came back up. No one, Duncan would swear, had physically touched the button, yet it had been depressed."*

The Cold War is back in this psi-techno suspense thriller where international aggressors use psychokinesis, astral projection and other psychic means to circumvent the U.S. intelligence network. When two routine communications satellite launches are inexplicably aborted at Vandenberg Air Force Base in California, one senator suspects paranormal influences. He calls in a writer, two parapsychologists and a psychic housewife—and The Committee is formed. Together, they piece together a sinister occult plot against the United States. The Committee then embarks on a supernatural adventure of a lifetime as they attempt to beat the enemy at its own game.

Llewellyn Psi-Fi Fiction Series
1-56718-100-7, 240 pgs., mass market                $4.99